The Boss's Baby Mistake

RAYE MORGAN

SILHOUETTE *Romance*

Published by Silhouette Books

America's Publisher of Contemporary Romance

To Marie Ferrarella.

Look under "friend" in the dictionary. I'm having your
name inserted as the first definition.

 SILHOUETTE BOOKS

ISBN 0-373-19499-4

THE BOSS'S BABY MISTAKE

Copyright © 2001 by Helen Conrad

All rights reserved. Except for use in any review, the reproduction
or utilization of this work in whole or in part in any form by any
electronic, mechanical or other means, now known or hereafter
invented, including xerography, photocopying and recording, or in
any information storage or retrieval system, is forbidden without
the written permission of the editorial office, Silhouette Books,
300 East 42nd Street, New York, NY 10017 U.S.A.

All characters in this book have no existence outside the imagination of
the author and have no relation whatsoever to anyone bearing the same
name or names. They are not even distantly inspired by any individual
known or unknown to the author, and all incidents are pure invention.

This edition published by arrangement with Harlequin Books S.A.

® and TM are trademarks of Harlequin Books S.A., used under license.
Trademarks indicated with ® are registered in the United States Patent
and Trademark Office, the Canadian Trade Marks Office and in other
countries.

Visit Silhouette at www.eHarlequin.com

Printed in U.S.A.

Her new boss's dark eyes were inscrutable when he spoke to her.

"You've got a baby boy coming in two months, and I know you want to make sure he gets here in good shape."

Gayle stared at him, frowning. He was practically a stranger. And yet he knew all about her situation, even the sex of the baby she was carrying. No one but the clinic doctors should know about what had happened. So how had Jack Marin known about her case?

Gayle wet her lips with her tongue and took a deep breath. "Mr. Marin…"

"Call me Jack."

"Jack…" She studied him, trying to get some answers from reading his face. But that wasn't easy. He merely cocked one dark eyebrow in amusement.

She blinked at him, totally at sea. "Jack, who, exactly, are you?"

His ebony-eyed gaze held hers. "Why, Gayle, I thought you knew. I'm the father of your baby."

Dear Reader,

As senior editor for the Silhouette Romance line, I'm lucky enough to get first peek at the stories we offer you each month. Each editor searches for stories with an emotional impact, that make us laugh or cry or feel tenderness and hope for a loving future. And we do this with *you,* the reader, in mind. We hope you continue to enjoy the variety each month as we take you from first love to forever....

Susan Meier's wonderful story of a hardworking single mom and the man who sweeps her off her feet is *Cinderella and the CEO.* In *The Boss's Baby Mistake,* Raye Morgan tells of a heroine who accidentally gets inseminated with her new boss's child! The fantasy stays alive with Carol Grace's *Fit for a Sheik* as a wedding planner's new client is more than she bargained for....

Valerie Parv always creates a strong alpha hero. In *Booties and the Beast,* Sam's the strong yet tender man. Julianna Morris's lighthearted yet emotional story *Meeting Megan Again* reunites two people who only *seem* mismatched. And finally Carolyn Greene's *An Eligible Bachelor* has a very special secondary character—along with a delightful hero and heroine!

Next month, look for our newest ROYALLY WED series with Stella Bagwell's *The Expectant Princess.* Marie Ferrarella astounds readers with *Rough Around the Edges*—her 100th title for Silhouette Books! And, of course, there will be more stories throughout the year chosen just for you.

Happy reading!

Mary-Theresa Hussey

Mary-Theresa Hussey
Senior Editor

Please address questions and book requests to:
Silhouette Reader Service
U.S.: 3010 Walden Ave., P.O. Box 1325, Buffalo, NY 14269
Canadian: P.O. Box 609, Fort Erie, Ont. L2A 5X3

RAYE MORGAN

has spent almost two decades, while writing over 50 novels, searching for the answer to that elusive question: just what is that special magic that happens when a man and a woman fall in love? Every time she thinks she has the answer, a new wrinkle pops up, necessitating another book! Meanwhile, after living in Holland, Guam, Japan and Washington, D.C., she currently makes her home in Southern California with her husband and two of her four boys.

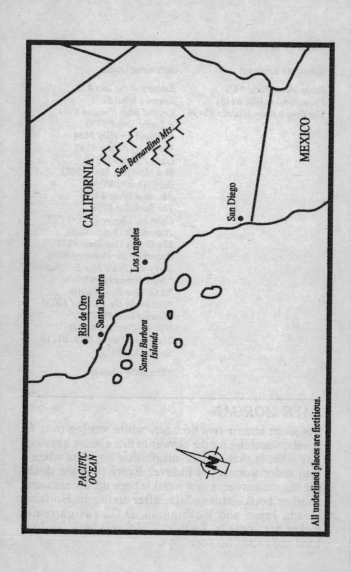

All underlined places are fictitious.

Chapter One

The voices were swirling around Gayle Smith, and at first they didn't make any sense. She frowned, trying to get this straight. The baby she was carrying wasn't her late husband's? How could this be?

"We are so sorry, Mrs. Smith. Nothing like this has ever happened here at Jollaire Medical Labs before."

She shook her head, as though she could shake some sense into it. They had to be wrong. This was impossible. But the faces that stared down at her all had such worried looks on them.

"The lab assistant involved has been fired...."

"If you would please sign this release form and..."

She winced and pulled back. The doctors were crowding her. She'd dealt with most of them over the long weeks of attempting to get pregnant, and she'd liked them all. They'd seemed caring and friendly. They'd been especially compassionate when her husband had died suddenly and left her alone to follow through on the childbearing plans they'd laid together. But now these people looked like strangers.

And she was alone. Without her husband here beside her to help make sense of this, without anyone in her corner, she felt badgered and isolated. A deep, lonesome feeling filled her soul, the same feeling she remembered from her childhood when she'd often been left alone in the isolated Alaskan cabin where she'd been raised. She winced and put her hands protectively over the rounded belly that held her child, fighting back that familiar feeling of desolation.

"We're here to help you in any way we can...."

She took a deep breath, steadying herself. This was no time to panic. She raised her hand automatically to smooth back her auburn curls, and the short, very round man in front of her flinched, as though he expected to be hit.

She stared at him. They had done something terrible. And now, what did they want from her?

"Please sign this form, right here by the X."

The voices were becoming more insistent, but this was no time to sign forms and make decisions. She could hardly think clearly. She had to get away from them all so she could think this through.

She rose from her chair, headed for the door and stumbled from the room, resisting their efforts to stop her.

A mistake. The words echoed in her head. *A mistake. A mistake.*

It didn't make sense. Things like this just didn't happen. No matter how they tried to explain it to her, she couldn't quite get her mind around it. This had to be—ha!—a mistake.

She almost released a slightly hysterical laugh, but she didn't get a chance to, because there was a great big man with very wide shoulders standing in her way. She looked up at him, blinking as she tried to make him out, because at first his face was obscured by the light spiking in from the bank of windows behind him, creating a halo effect.

"Mrs. Smith?" the man was saying, looking down at her.

His face came into focus. She looked at him blankly, uncomprehending. He wasn't wearing a white coat and she didn't remember having seen him here before, so she didn't think he was one of the doctors. Was he going to apologize for the mistake, too?

Maybe not. He didn't look as scared as the others did. In fact, he was gazing at her with dark eyes that gleamed with a certain calm confidence, a sense of assurance she only wished she had at the moment.

He took her hand in both of his, as though to comfort and protect her. His touch was solid, strong, and it filled her with a sense of warmth.

"Mrs. Smith, I'd like to help you. My name is Jack Marin."

Jack Marin. The name was not familiar, but his eyes were kind as they met hers. That was good enough for her right now. Besides that, she thought with a small, guilty thrill, he was awfully good-looking. That never hurt.

"Mr. Marin!" One of the men in the white coats was yelling at him, his face turning red from the effort, his voice getting louder and louder. "This is highly irregular! You shouldn't have any contact with this woman!"

"Mr. Marin," said another of the doctors sternly. He had a large walrus mustache, which added immensely to his authority. "I must ask you to leave at once. I will have to call security if you do not vacate these premises immediately."

Jack Marin dropped her hand as he faced them, standing his ground. "You can call anyone you like," he told them calmly, his dark eyes becoming cold as they turned toward the doctors. "You're the ones who are responsible for this disaster. This lady is the victim of your mismanagement. I don't think you want that getting out, now do you?"

"Mr. Marin, you have no right—"

He held up a hand to stop the protests. "Doctors, if you want to discuss this further, we'll see you in court."

The doctors looked stunned, and Gayle almost felt sorry for them. Her new friend was turning out to be very handy to have around, and he seemed to know how to push all the right buttons. She took a step closer to him. At least there was one person here on her side.

He must be a lawyer, she thought with a certain sense of irony. *He must have heard about this mistake, and came to give me legal counsel.*

"Mrs. Smith needs time to assimilate what you've disclosed to her," Jack Marin told them, taking her arm as though she'd already hired him on. "She needs to sit down somewhere and think over whether or not she's going to sue the pants off you bunch of frauds.''

He looked down into Gayle's face and smiled reassuringly. She soaked up his strength from his smile and held her head high.

"Good day, gentlemen," he said as he began to lead her toward the elevator. "We'll be in touch."

The doctors were milling about in frustration and murmuring among themselves, obviously at a loss as to what they would do next, but Gayle hardly noticed. In a daze, she let Jack escort her onto the elevator. In mere seconds, the doors closed and she couldn't see the doctors any longer. She blinked, wishing she could believe this was all a bad dream.

"I know the perfect place to get some privacy," her rescuer told her smoothly. "La Paix, a little French restaurant, is right across the street. Great food, quiet atmosphere. Just what you need."

She knew the place to be one of the better restaurants in Rio de Oro, a medium-sized town on the central California Coast. She gave him a shaky smile, glad he was there. She knew she was going to have to make decisions regarding this debacle on her own, but it was a comfort to have someone help her through the early stages. She'd always been fairly solitary, but she'd never been so completely alone in the world before. She'd always lived with her father, and then, once he'd died, she had married and lived with her husband. It had only been a few months since she'd lost him in turn, and she wasn't totally used to standing alone yet.

She had been doing pretty well up to now. In fact, she'd been surprised at how easily she'd made the transition from wife to widow, despite a lot of obstacles that had been thrown her way, even before this latest bombshell. In fact, she'd been pretty proud of herself and the way she was weathering the storm. But that was before she'd been hit with the news that her baby's father was a stranger.

Her new friend didn't say any more as they descended and made their way out of the building. She was glad of that. She didn't feel like making small talk. She glanced over at him, met his jet-black gaze and felt a quick frisson of electricity shoot through her system.

She looked away immediately, blushing. That was very odd, she thought. She didn't react that way to men. Never. Never ever. It had to be because of the strange circumstances...and the heightened emotions of the situation...and the fact that he had the most intense dark eyes she'd ever gazed into.

She tried to dismiss it from her mind and pretty much succeeded for a time. He took her arm again as they crossed the street, and she didn't let it throw her. He seemed very large and very protective. She liked that. It would be such a luxury to be able to relax and let him take some of the worry off her shoulders. She knew she couldn't do that—but the thought was certainly tempting.

"Do you always give your clients this sort of first-class service?" she murmured as they reached the curb.

"My clients?" he said absently, steering her toward the double doors. He threw a quizzical look her way, as though doing a quick scan to make sure she wasn't going woozy on him. "You need to sit down and take it easy," he told her, opening the door to let her in. "Then we'll talk."

The little French restaurant had frilly white curtains and dimly lit, individual booths. The waiters wore black suits and the maître d' wore a tuxedo. The music was classical and very soft, the ambience peaceful and serene. Gayle loved the place immediately.

The maître d' led them through the restaurant to a private section toward the back. Gayle slid into her side of the booth and sat back against the velveteen upholstery. The air was cool, the music sweet, the light filtered. She began to relax and, at the same time, felt her strength begin to return. She even felt strong enough to risk another look into her rescuer's eyes. Looking across the table, she prepared herself, then smiled at him and was chagrinned to feel that tingle again. What was the matter with her, anyway?

She had to admit he was one of the most attractive men she'd ever met. She wondered fleetingly if she'd ever met him before, but she couldn't place him. And it didn't matter. He knew what had happened, it seemed, and he was ready to help her.

The waiter set a tall, frosted glass of something lime-green in front of her that Mr. Marin must have ordered when she wasn't paying attention, and she took a sip, savoring its light, sherbety taste. She was definitely calming down. But the situation still seemed surreal.

"Feeling better?" Jack asked her.

She folded her hands before her on the white linen tablecloth and studied him for a long moment before answering. He was a classically handsome man and his dark eyes seemed warm and kind. He wore a crisp white shirt, open at the neck, with his shirt-sleeves rolled up to just below his elbows. She could see that he was a strong man. His chest looked muscular, and so did his forearms.

He was the sort of man a woman could easily fall for, she decided. The sort of man a girl might fantasize making love to. She found her gaze dropping to explore the tanned chest exposed by his open shirt, and felt a hint of that electricity again.

Quickly, she looked away. But his image stayed in her mind. There was something about him, something with a hint of the wild and rugged, that didn't fit with his being a lawyer. She could see him more as some sort of outdoorsman, scaling mountains rather than dominating courtrooms.

"I am feeling better," she told him. "It was a shock to find out...." Her voice trailed off as she put her hands on her rounded belly. She couldn't say it aloud yet. She was carrying a baby who was suddenly a bit of a stranger to her. Everything she had believed to be true about her child's conception had been shattered. It was going to take some getting used to. "The question is, what do I do now?"

He shrugged his wide shoulders and narrowed his eyes, assessing her. "Sue them. You'll make millions."

She groaned. "Right. And the case will drag through the courts for years for the hope of a settlement that may never come to pass."

He raised one dark eyebrow. "It sounds like you've already had that experience," he noted.

She lifted her shoulders casually. She didn't want

to remember the people who had sued her after her father's death, claiming he had swindled them. She'd been too young to deal with it all, and Hank, her father's business partner, had stepped in and guided her through the legal maze at the time. She'd married him, partly in gratitude, and he'd taken care of everything... But she didn't like to let her mind dwell on those days.

"Something close," she said. "And I'll never go through that again." She paused as the waiter set a plate of cheese and crackers on the table, then she gave Jack a wavering smile. "I'm sorry Mr....Marin, was it? You've been very kind, but I won't be suing."

She expected him to look disappointed, but instead, his gaze sharpened. "I don't think you should make a firm decision about that until you've had some time to let this sink in." He hesitated, his gaze dropping to what he could see of her belly. "Everything is going all right, isn't it?"

"Oh yes. I'm fine. It's been a relatively easy pregnancy, or so they tell me." She said a quick, silent prayer of thanks for that. "I'm almost at seven months. It won't be long now."

His dark eyes were inscrutable. "Good. You've got a healthy little boy coming and I know you want to do everything you can to make sure he gets here in good shape."

She stared at him, frowning. The man was a complete stranger. And yet he knew all about her situation, even the sex of the baby she was carrying.

It finally dawned on her that no one else but the doctors should know about what had happened.

She'd been assuming he was a lawyer, but how had he known about her case? And why had he shown up out of the blue just when she was there? Now that she was thinking more clearly, she began to see that this wasn't really making a lot of sense.

She wet her lips with her tongue and took a deep breath. "Mr. Marin..."

His dark eyes met hers. "Call me Jack."

"Jack...I told you I'm not interested in suing." She awaited his response, trying to get some answers from reading his face.

But that wasn't easy. Instead of trying to talk her into reconsidering, he merely nodded. "I'm glad. I hate that kind of thing, too."

She shook her head, perplexed. "But...aren't you a lawyer?"

One dark eyebrow cocked in amusement. "A lawyer? No, whatever gave you that idea?"

She blinked at him, now totally at sea. "Who are you?"

His clear-eyed gaze held hers. "Why, Gayle, I thought you knew. I'm the father of your baby."

Chapter Two

Gayle's chest felt as though it would explode. Her hands clenched the edge of the table and she stared at Jack, aghast.

"What?" she said breathlessly, her eyes round as saucers. "What?"

"I'm sorry. I thought you understood, or I would have explained sooner."

Her heart skipped a beat and then began to pound like a drum, shooting adrenaline through her system. She needed to escape—again. The phrase "Out of the frying pan, into the fire" came to mind. She reached for her purse and slid out of the booth. "Stay away from me," she warned, glaring at the man. "Keep your distance."

He was shaking his head as he gazed at her, and the look of sympathetic understanding was quickly replaced by an expression of cool exasperation. "I'm sorry, Gayle," he said, just as calm and sure with her as he'd been with the doctors. "I'm afraid I can't do that. You're carrying something that belongs to me."

She stood at the edge of the table, staring down at him. "What?" she said, outraged. "I...you have no right..."

"Oh yes, I do." He gestured with a nod of his head. "Sit back down. We need to deal with this in a rational manner."

Rational? What was rational about this impossible situation? She shook her head. "I'm going home," she announced firmly, though she still hadn't started away from the table. Something about the man was holding her here, even though he wasn't touching her. "If you have anything to tell me, you can write me a letter."

He sighed, his dark eyes clouding. "Calm down," he told her. "You're not going anywhere. I definitely can't let you drive yourself home when you're so upset."

She blinked, clutching her purse to her chest. "*Let me?* What possible business is it of yours?"

"It is very much my business. You're carrying my child. I don't want that baby hurt." He made a gesture of forbearance and gave her a hard look. "If you insist on passing up the great food this place has to offer, I'm going to have to do the same, and drive you home myself."

She stared at him as he unfolded his long, muscular frame and stood before her. Gayle was tall for a woman, but she only came up to his shoulder. He started to reach out to take her arm, but she jerked away, and the look in her eyes seemed to stop him from trying again. He looked down at her with a half smile, more bemused than angry.

"Gayle, we are going to talk this through. We can either do it at your house or we can do it here. Since you hardly know me, I would think you would prefer it in a public place." He shrugged. "But the location is up to you. You choose."

Something visceral told her to believe everything he said. She wasn't used to dealing with this sort of man. Her father had been a lovable teddy bear who would shower his daughter with presents—even if it often was to make up for having left her alone so much. Her husband had been hesitant and diffident, willing to let her take the lead in most choices and judgments.

But this man, this Jack Marin, was a different breed entirely. She could see that he was tough, that he was used to making decisions swiftly and following through on threats. She searched his ebony eyes and couldn't find any hint of uncertainty. If she didn't let him drive her, he would follow her home. She knew that as well as if he'd told her so. He wanted to discuss this issue between them, and it was going to be discussed. Simple as that.

Slowly, she sank back down into her seat at the table. She wasn't about to give in to anything he wanted. But for now, she was going to play along and see just exactly what his demands were going to be.

"All right," she said evenly, lifting her chin. "Let's talk."

Jack slid back into his own seat and looked across the table at her, doing a quick reassessment of his

situation. He knew what he wanted. He wanted his
son. That was as important to him as anything had
ever been. Ordinarily, he was used to making things
happen the way he wanted them to. But in this instance, he didn't have the control he would have
liked. What he yearned for was inside the body of
another human being. That made it tricky.

He watched her, studied her, glad that she was
easy on the eyes. Then he looked away quickly when
he realized what he was doing. He wondered if she'd
noticed. But he couldn't help it. This was the mother
of his son. He wanted to become familiar with every
detail.

He liked her lustrous auburn hair. And her wide
blue eyes. And the dimple that had disappeared now
that she wasn't smiling any longer. He wanted to ask
her about her family background, about illnesses, talents, foibles. What was her father like? Any insanity
in her family? Curly hair? Twins? Musical ability?
All the questions inside him he would have to hold
back for now. If he pushed too hard, she would only
retreat again. He had to play this just right.

It seemed it was going to take skill and tenacity
to end up with what he wanted. This elegantly tall
and graceful woman sitting across from him was no
pushover. There was spirit in those azure eyes and
evidence of a certain fire in the set of her lush, beautiful mouth. But he'd dealt with women before. He
could handle her, too.

The advantage he figured he had was that he knew
from experience women were not to be trusted. As
far as he was concerned, it went right back to Adam

and Eve, and it was the same story over and over again. The woman held out temptation, the gullible man reached for it and she casually cut him off at the knees. It was a pattern that had been repeated often in his own family. His mother had put his father through hell, then left him. Not having learned from example, Jack himself had married the girl of his dreams, he'd thought, only to be plummeted by the reality—a woman who promised everything and left him with less than nothing. He'd finally wised up, when it was too late. But that wouldn't ever happen to him again. He would make sure of that.

There were relationships in this world that truly mattered to him. He even had a sister whom he adored. But they were the exceptions. He'd found that most women had to be watched every moment. They were like Siamese cats, sleek and beautiful—and ready to sell you out for a better offer at any time. You had to watch your back.

"I don't bite," he told Gayle after they had sat in silence for a good two or three minutes. "At least, not until I get to know a woman better."

She glared at him, just to let him know she didn't appreciate his jokes at a time like this, and he grinned back at her.

"Hey, we're both in this together," he said, his dark eyes sparkling with a brittle light. "Why are you looking at me like I'm the enemy?"

She held his gaze. Funny how his smile didn't seem to reach his eyes any longer. "You've got to admit, you're the closest thing to an enemy I've got," she said evenly. "I was living my life very peacefully when you intruded."

He studied her face. "Would you rather not have known what happened?"

She thought for a moment, considering. "I don't know. Maybe." She fidgeted with her fork, then looked up at him again. "Just exactly what is it that you want?" she asked bravely, though she was completely terrified of the answer she was sure he would give.

He didn't answer directly. Instead, he began working with the cheese and crackers, and said, "I didn't plan to have things turn out this way. This was no more in my game plan than it was in yours. I contracted for a service, nothing more." He put down the cheese knife and looked into her eyes, his own hard as stones. "The outcome is what is important to me. I intend to end up with my son. That's all."

She suddenly felt short of breath. She'd known this, of course. It had been obvious from the moment he'd told her who he was. But she couldn't accept it. The thought that he could even imagine she might consider letting him have her baby... She would never give up her child. Didn't he know that? Couldn't he guess? Looking toward the exit, she longed to get away.

"Bottom line," he said almost too softly, "is that you've got something we both want."

She swallowed hard and looked away again, avoiding his gaze. He was right. She did have something they both wanted. And yet, at the moment, she wasn't sure what she really had.

This was no longer the little boy she had imagined. There was no chance now that he would have Hank's gray eyes, or his offbeat sense of humor, or his slender build. The father of her child was entirely different now. He would have bits and pieces of the large, strong, arrogant man across from her. Would that have any effect on how she felt about the baby? She didn't think so…but how could she know for sure at this point?

Her hands went to her belly again, fingers spread as though to sense any new vibrations. She felt a small movement, then a definite kick against one palm. And a warm wave of such overwhelming love swept through her that she almost had to smile. No, it made no difference. She would love her son no matter what he looked like, what his personality turned out to be. How could a woman carry a baby for nine months and not love it? A feeling of peace came over her. She knew what the outcome of this problem would be. Now all she had to do was find a way to get this man to accept it.

"This is really pointless," she told him simply. "I'll never give up my baby. I don't care what kind of contract you have. That's between you and the lab. It has nothing to do with me."

He merely gave her one of those smiles that left his eyes cool and confident. "Would you like another sherbet drink?"

She shook her head. "No, thank you. Plying me with fancy drinks won't help change my mind, you know."

She sighed. He wasn't going to get what he wanted, but he was going to make her fight for every inch, that was clear. He wanted a son. But he hadn't said anything about a wife, or asked what *she* wanted. Gayle had a sudden premonition. If there was a wife involved, he would have mentioned her by now. What if there wasn't a wife?

"Are you married?" she asked abruptly.

A look of pure challenge flashed in his dark eyes. "No," he said at last, reluctantly.

That was what she'd thought. What a mystery this man was. Still, she had to admit he was awfully good-looking. Despite the antagonism between them, she felt a strong pull of attraction. She remembered the feeling she'd had when her gaze had met his in the elevator, and she knew that electricity was simmering just below the surface even now. If she dropped her guard, she would feel it again. There was something masculine in him that she couldn't help but respond to. But she had to remember that he was the enemy.

She studied him from under her lashes. His dark hair was cut fairly short, as though he was trying to tame a tendency toward crisp curls that she could detect along his neckline. His profile was strong, and his dark eyes were deep and gorgeous. But the feature that struck her most strongly was his mouth. He had the sexiest mouth she'd ever seen. It looked like it had been created just for kissing. The thought of kissing it sent a sudden surge of sensation through her and she dropped her gaze quickly, willing herself not to blush. That would be a sign of weakness she couldn't risk.

She finally glanced back into his eyes and congratulated herself on how cool and calm she'd managed to be. "Why don't you explain just exactly what you want with a child when you have no wife to help you raise him?" she demanded.

His expression was guarded. "I will explain that to you. But not yet." He waited a moment as the waiter refilled their water glasses. "We need to get to know each other first."

He made this sound like a long-term relationship. She had no intention of letting it go any longer than this day, this meal. "And how do you propose we go about doing that?" she asked impatiently.

He looked very sure of himself. "We'll eat a meal. Look at each other across the table. Talk about this and that." He let a glint of humor appear in his gaze. "Give each other a smile now and then."

So that was it. Her mouth turned down in a cynical frown. "You're counting on your charm to bowl me over, aren't you?"

He laughed, and it lit up his dark face. "No, Gayle. I have a feeling it would take more than my charm to bowl *you* over." His smile faded. "I'm counting on facts and logic."

Facts and logic. *Facts and logic!*

"You know, this whole thing is still very unreal and very scary to me," she said after the waiter took their order and walked away. "Just a few hours ago I was carrying my husband's child. And now…" Her voice wavered and trailed off as a surge of emotion surprised her.

He cleared his throat. "I heard about what happened to your husband. I'm very sorry."

"Are you?"

He frowned at the question. "Yes. Of course."

She took a deep breath and continued. "I thought I still had a piece of my husband—" Her voice broke and she shook her head, annoyed with herself. The one thing she didn't want to do was to cry in front of him. But she couldn't stop herself from adding softly, "Now I don't have anything."

He stared at her and had to admit she was getting to him. He saw her huge eyes brim with sparkling tears, then watched as she forced them back. He felt like he should do something. But what? Take her in his arms? That had a certain appeal, but he didn't think it would be appropriate at this point. His ex-wife had used the tears ploy so often he'd actually grown hardened to it. But Gayle was either a very good actress or she really was upset.

Abruptly, he felt contrite. Hell, the woman had lost her husband, and now she was facing the prospect of losing her baby. Of course she was upset. What was he thinking? Maybe he should…well, reach out and take her hand, at least. He looked at it, lying on the table, the fingers long and delicate, the nails rounded and silvery-pink. And suddenly he wanted to hold it, wanted to comfort her. He started to reach out, but at the same moment, she put her hand in her lap.

"I am really very sorry for your loss," he said instead, after giving her a moment to compose herself.

When her gaze met his again, her eyes were clear. "Thank you," she said calmly.

He felt a sense of relief. She was okay. She wasn't going to break down. He was glad of that, not wanting to go soft on her. He had to keep his mind on what this was all about. She was very pretty, and seemed actually to be a very nice person. He liked her spirit, liked the way she smoothed back her beautiful mahogany hair and set her full lips, as though she was making up her mind to do something that was difficult for her. Under any other circumstances, he might even be attracted to her. Except that—hell, how could he forget?—she was seven months pregnant. Funny how he seemed to lose sight of that when he looked at her. He'd never been attracted to a pregnant woman before. He wasn't sure that he liked it.

"This is hard on you right now," he said gruffly. "And I'm sorry for that. But we don't have the luxury of a lot of time. We've got a baby coming and we have to get things settled. Because...you see, what you do have is...part of me."

Her eyes widened and he added quickly, "I know that isn't what you want. But it's the truth. And you know, if you think about it, that should make this so much simpler for you."

"Simpler? How?"

"The baby you're carrying isn't what you wanted any longer. But it is exactly what I want." He saw the shock in her eyes and he added, "I'm sure you'll marry again. There will be other chances for you to have...well, another baby." And he watched for her response, hoping to see if his arguments were making any sort of dent in her resolve.

She was pale and looked furious. *There, you see?* he thought with resignation. *Logic and facts never seem to go over very well with women. Go figure.*

"You're suggesting I resign myself to having another baby?" she echoed, the outrage flashing in her eyes. Looking at Jack, she forced herself to hold back her anger and make conversation instead of blowing up at him. "What do you do for a living?" she asked shortly.

"I'm a geologist," he responded. "How about you?"

"I'm a Web designer," she said absently. "But I'm unemployed right now." She looked at him. "How about a short biographical sketch?"

"Why not?" he said, leaning back and folding his arms across his chest. "I was born on the family ranch in Santa Ynez, a ranch my father still works today. It was originally a Spanish land grant, established in 1820. A lot of Marins have come down the pike since then, a lot have worked that ranch." He threw her a direct look. "Seven generations of Marins have lived in the Santa Ynez Valley. I plan to make it eight."

He went on as their food was served and they began to eat, talking about growing up on the ranch, about his rebellious decision to go into geology instead of ranching, his father's anger at his choice. He gave her a sketchy picture of his failed marriage and let her know he had no intention of repeating a mistake like that ever again.

She listened quietly, completely forgetting her anger. She ate sporadically from her salad and sipped her iced tea, but she didn't taste a thing. His words were simple, but she was touched by the raw yearning she thought she could hear in them.

When he finished, she gave him a short version of her own life, how she'd been raised in Alaska and had married her father's best friend and business partner right after her father's death. How they had moved to California and she'd gone to technical school rather than college and learned computer programming and Web design. How her husband's health had failed right when they had finally succeeded in conceiving a child. Or thought they had.

And all the time, she was wondering how any woman could have left a man like this. But of course, there had to be things about him that she didn't have a clue about. And maybe she was being a sucker, falling for his sad tale. Maybe. All she knew was, if she'd had a chance at a man like Jack when she was younger, she'd have leaped tall buildings to get at it. Or climbed tall mountains, considering she'd been in Alaska. She'd married so young, and after such an isolated life, she'd never had a chance to do any dating. And later, even though she'd met many more men at work, she'd never felt comfortable with the sort of flirting other women seemed to fall into naturally with any attractive man. She was a married woman, after all.

Then she it hit her; she wasn't married at all, not anymore.

Chapter Three

Gayle took a long, cool drink of water and cleared her throat. There didn't seem to be anything left to say. Jack seemed to feel it, too. This conversation had run its course for now.

He paid the bill and they both rose to leave. As they walked out, he put a hand gently behind her neck to lead her to the street. She jumped when she first felt his touch, but he didn't withdraw his hand and so she didn't say anything. Still, it was definitely disturbing, making her skin so sensitive she had to consciously ignore it to keep from reacting, and she was relieved when he let her go once on the sidewalk.

"Where are you parked?" he asked. She told him and they started toward the parking structure.

"I don't really need an escort," she told him lightly. "I've been getting my car from parking lots for a long time now. Haven't had a problem yet."

He smiled but didn't say anything, and kept right on walking with her. They had to go past a row of pink oleanders and through the old Spanish plaza with its worn bricks and colorful tile. There was a bench in front of a fountain ahead, the cascading water sparkling silvery in the sunlight. He watched her for a moment. He didn't know why, but he didn't want to let her go just yet. He told himself it was because they still hadn't settled anything and they still needed to talk, but he knew it was more than that.

"Gayle, wait a moment." He took her arm, stopping her. "Come sit with me over there on that bench. We still have a few things to talk about."

She stared into his eyes for a moment, and he knew she wanted to go, wanted to get away from him. He couldn't blame her. He'd completely disrupted her life. To her, he was nothing but a problem that she wished would evaporate. He was going to have to convince her that he was not going to disappear from the scene anytime soon.

Finally she nodded and started toward the bench. He came with her, reaching out with his handkerchief to sweep off the leaves before letting her seat herself. She brushed by him as she did so, her hair floating behind her and leaving her scent in the air. He took a deep breath, wanting more of it. She smelled like flowers, like sunshine and happiness. As he sat down beside her, he had to resist the impulse to touch her hair.

She turned to look at him and her eyes were saying, "Make this quick, mister, I want to get going."

He grimaced. "Gayle, you're going to have to realize, whether you like it or not, we're tied together."

She swallowed. "I...I'm not sure I know what you mean," she said faintly.

"You have a part of me inside you. I want it back."

Her eyes hardened and she faced him with her head held high. "But the only way for you to get it back is to take part of me," she said boldly. "And I won't give it up."

He searched her eyes. She wasn't going to yield. He had to admire her for that. But it didn't help his cause.

She saw the consternation in his eyes and impulsively, reached out to touch his arm. "Believe me, if there was anything I could do to make this right for you, I would." She shook her head. "But don't you see? You can't ask me to give up my baby. That just isn't going to happen."

She was prepared to accept anger from him, or bitterness, or even frustrated rage. But instead he smiled. And then he reached out and gently touched her cheek with the backs of his fingers, while his dark gaze slowly scanned her features.

Suddenly her heart was thumping in her chest, and she wasn't sure if it was because he completely discounted the strength of her will, or because a very attractive man was touching her. Either way, she knew she was in trouble.

But he was already drawing back, reaching into his pocket. "Here's my home phone number," he said, jotting it down on the back of one of his busi-

ness cards. "And my address." He handed her the
card. "Let me have your number."

"Why?" she asked suspiciously.

"So I can harass you with crank calls from dusk
till dawn," he said, giving her a look of pure exasperation. "Come on, Gayle. I need your number."

Sighing, she wrote down her number on another
of his cards.

"There," she said, handing it over. "See how I
trust you?"

A faint smile played with the corners of his mouth
as he pocketed the card. "Trust is a precious thing,"
he said. "Precious and rare."

For the first time, she recognized the streak of bitterness in him, the source of the wary distrust that
so often filled his eyes even when his lips were smiling. She wondered if his ex-wife had turned him into
such a hard man, or if it was a trait he'd always had.

"Why did you decide to have the artificial insemination?" Jack asked her suddenly.

She looked at him, startled. The question seemed
too blunt, too personal.

"Why did you?" she countered.

He hesitated. "I wanted a son," he said at last.
"And I didn't want another wife."

She opened her mouth to ask more, but he was
already shaking his head. "I told you I would explain
it all to you at some point, but I don't want to go
into detail right now." He raised one eyebrow.
"Your turn."

She took a deep breath. "We decided on artificial
insemination for the usual reason. We tried the rou-

tine way. It didn't work.'' And she set her lips. If he
could withhold details, so could she.

But he wasn't asking for any. "So you thought
you'd let professionals handle it," he commented casually, sitting back with his elbows hanging over the
back of the bench, looking at the fountain. His legs
were stretched out in front of him, the wool fabric
of his slacks pulled taut by the muscles of his thighs.

Gayle noticed, then silently scolded herself for noticing.

"How did you get the name of these clowns across
the street?" he asked.

"Through work. We have a health representative
who does referrals.'' She sighed. ''They came very
well recommended.''

He nodded. "I researched the field extensively before I decided upon that clinic. They have a very
good reputation." He gazed at her speculatively.
"But I thought you said you were unemployed."

"Laid off." She pushed her hair back behind her
ear. She didn't want to think about that. She had
enough problems on her plate right now. "Just recently."

"Sorry. But you would have had to quit, anyway.
The baby…"

"I also have to eat," she said crisply. This situation wasn't like it had been when her father died and
the debts were piled to the ceiling. Still, she didn't
have a lot in savings. She had been planning to spend
this afternoon job hunting, but that window of opportunity was fast closing. "I'm signed up with Top
Techs, a temporary employment agency, but they

haven't called me with anything yet. I'm going to have to find something soon, though."

"Listen," he said, turning toward her on the bench. "I can help you. Money is no object. Just—"

"No!" She stared at him as though he'd suggested something horrible. "Never. I will not take money from you."

"Gayle, I'm the baby's father."

She wanted to close her eyes and cover her ears. "How do I know that? I don't have any proof that anything you've said about all this is true. For all I know, you made it up."

"You can check with the clinic. They'll have to let you see the documentation. Your husband's sample was accidentally destroyed and mine was taken out of turn. You'll be convinced. I was."

He was quiet for a moment, then he turned toward her and gazed into her eyes. "You know something? I'm sorry things didn't work out for you and your husband. But for me, I have to admit, things have worked out pretty well."

"What are you talking about?"

"You. I think you're just about what I would have ordered up as a mother for my child, if you had been in the mix when I had to make a choice."

She didn't know whether to laugh or cry, but he went on anyway. "You're smart, courageous, compassionate." His eyes darkened. "And you're very beautiful."

She gasped. "Beautiful?" He hadn't said it as a casual compliment. He'd said it with conviction, as though he really meant it. Just the way he'd said it made her tremble inside.

"Yes. Beautiful." He took a strand of her hair and curled it around his forefinger, and the way he moved as he did so, slowly, provocatively, left her breathless. "Hasn't anyone ever called you beautiful before?"

"Never," she whispered. And it was true.

"What? Didn't your husband speak English?"

She felt she had to defend him. "He...well, he wasn't very verbal about things like that." Hank had never been very romantic. He'd loved her. He'd put her on a pedestal. But he hadn't wanted to touch her very often.

She knew without having to analyze it that Jack would have been a very different husband. She barely knew him and already she sensed he could be a passionate lover. Her heart was beating a wild dance in her chest. He was too close. She could feel the heat from his body. And his fingers tugging on her hair made her think of things she shouldn't be thinking.

"Gayle," he said softly, "you're an exceptionally beautiful woman. And what's more, even though you're seven months pregnant, you're sexy as hell."

She felt as though she were drowning in his dark eyes. He was going to kiss her. Oh, she hoped so! She held her breath, waiting for his mouth to cover hers. She wanted to feel his lips so badly, she thought she would die without it.

But luckily that was a delusion, because he didn't kiss her at all. For just a moment, his gaze devoured hers, and he came ever closer. She waited, heart beating like a drum. But after a few excruciating seconds, he drew back and suddenly was acting as though nothing had happened.

"Anyway," he said casually, looking away, "the point is, we've got a mutual interest here. We both want you to have a calm, happy pregnancy. We both want our baby to be as healthy as possible. Agreed?"

Our baby. The words shocked her back to reality. She looked at him, wondering if she'd imagined everything that had happened in the last few moments. He didn't seem to think a thing of it. A flash of anger spiked through her, but she would die before she'd let him see how disappointed she was. "Yes," she said faintly. "Now I've got to get home...."

"All right," he said agreeably. "It is getting late."

They rose and he walked with her into the parking structure at the edge of the plaza. She avoided looking at him. She was going to go home and forget she'd ever met him! If only she could...

"There's my car," she said, pointing out her elderly blue compact as they approached it.

Jack frowned. "Are you sure this thing is safe?" he asked, running his finger over the faded hood.

"It's fine," she told him, unlocking the door. "I've had it for years."

Shoving his hands into his pockets, he watched her get into the car. "That's what I'm afraid of," he said grumpily. "Cars only have so many miles to give, you know. This one looks like it's about hit its limit."

He was worried about the baby, she knew. She gave him a patient look and started her engine, rolling down her window so that she could say goodbye. He bent down, leaning his hand on her car door.

"Have you named him?" he asked softly.

Her hand went protectively to her rounded belly. It felt odd to answer his question. She'd never told anyone other than Hank. "Yes," she said. "His name is going to be Michael."

"Michael," he said, pronouncing it slowly, rolling the name on his tongue as though to savor it. "I like that."

So glad you approve, she wanted to say, spiced with plenty of sarcasm. But she bit back the retort and found herself saying instead, "I call him Mikey right now."

Jack grinned, and she frowned, wishing she'd kept that to herself. He rose from his position against the door and she put the car in reverse.

"Thank you for lunch," she said formally, backing out of her parking space. "Talk to you soon."

"You can bet on it," he told her, standing with his hands in his pockets and watching her from under dark brows.

With a wave of her hand, she drove off and left him gazing after her.

There was still part of the afternoon left, but it was useless trying to get anything done. Gayle couldn't bend over well enough to work on her gardening. She couldn't read or listen to music or watch television. Her mind was stuck in overdrive, thinking about nothing but the situation she'd found herself thrust into. And the baby seemed to be running on a treadmill. She'd never known him to be so active.

In the evening, she thought of calling Chareen Wolf, her one good friend who had children. She'd been talking to Chareen a lot over the last few months. Gayle'd often needed advice and some morale boosting. Chareen's blunt attitude struck just the right note for her. Yes, she would call Chareen, tell her about what had happened, get her down-to-earth advice. She went to the phone with a feeling of relief, dialing quickly. But no one answered the telephone, and then she remembered that Chareen was out of town on a business trip.

Suddenly Gayle felt even more isolated than she had before. There was no one she could call, no one she could talk to. Her other friends had never been pregnant. Only one of them was even married. They really couldn't understand what she was going through. She had no one she could tell about what had happened, about the situation she was in...about Jack Marin and his powerful effect on her. She had never felt so alone.

She was dealing with so many things that she felt like a swimmer going down for the third time. Besides the issues with the baby, there was something else. Why had she reacted so strongly to the man? Why had she wanted him to kiss her?

Because she had wanted exactly that. She wanted it now, when she thought about him, about his handsome face, his strong mouth. It was as though she'd found out something she hadn't known about before, as though she'd awakened to a need that had been slumbering inside her all these years. She'd never had real passion with a man.

But even thinking about it felt wrong. After all, she was beyond that, wasn't she? She'd been mar-

ried. She was pregnant. This wasn't the right time.
And Jack Marin definitely wasn't the right man.

She sat in the living room for the next hour and
flipped through a magazine, but a new thought was
tormenting her like a pesky fly. Was this the way it
was going to be? Was she really going to be alone
with every decision, every new worry about her baby
once he was born? She had no family to fall back
on. She couldn't bother Chareen all the time. As the
night got later, her mood grew darker, and she began
to see the future as a deep, black emptiness yawning
before her, filled with demands and decisions.

The only thing she could think of to lift her spirits
was to call someone. Maybe Kyra Symington was
home. Gayle called the number her friend shared
with her new husband, but she only got the answering machine. She tried Ann Marie Hope's, and then
Tracy Martin's, with the same result. She began to
wonder if all her friends had gone somewhere together, forgetting all about her.

Suddenly the phone rang while her hand was still
on the receiver, making her jump. Quickly she answered, grateful for the promise of human contact.

"Hello?"

"Hi."

It was him. She knew his voice immediately, and
for some crazy reason, her pulse began to race.

"Hi," she said. "Is something wrong?"

"No. I just wanted to check if this number was
correct."

There was a hint of amusement in his voice, but
she wasn't sure what that meant. "Why would I give

you a wrong number?'' she asked, feeling a bit defensive.

"To avoid hearing from me?"

She hesitated, still not sure if he were goading her or laughing.

"How are you feeling?" he asked casually, before she had time to think of something to say.

It would be nice to think he cared about her, but she knew he only cared about the baby. And she couldn't blame him. It was only natural and logical. Still...

"Fine," she said, but again she knew she sounded defensive. And she really didn't mean to.

"Good." He paused, then continued. "I'd like to see you tomorrow."

She shook her head, even though he couldn't see that. "No, impossible. I'm busy tomorrow."

"All day?"

"Well..." The truth was, she was only hoping to be busy. "I told you, I've signed up with Top Techs. I'm expecting a call first thing in the morning, and then I'll be working all day."

"Top Techs, huh?" His voice sounded ironic, but perhaps that was just her being overly sensitive. "They're a good agency. I've used them in the past."

"How interesting." There wasn't anything else to say, was there? She tensed, hoping he wasn't going to start in again on how she should give up her baby to him. But he didn't do that.

"Okay," he said. "I just want to let you know I'm here if you need me. Really. Any time of day or night. I will make sure you can always get hold of me.''

For the baby's sake, of course. "I'm not sure if I feel comforted or threatened by that," she said dryly, then immediately regretted sounding churlish. After all, he was being very nice. And that was a good thing, even if it was for an ulterior motive.

He was silent so long, she wondered if he'd hung up and she'd missed it. "Gayle," he said at last. "Are you sure you're okay?"

She sighed. "Yes. Yes, I'm fine. It's just...well, it's been a rough day."

He was silent for another minute, then he said, "Gayle, I've got a question for you."

Her fingers tightened on the receiver. "What's that?" she asked him, trying not to let him hear the apprehension in her voice.

"How do you know when an elephant's been in your refrigerator?"

She blinked. "What?"

"You can see the footprint on your pizza," he said, his voice impassively earnest. "How can you tell that an elephant's getting ready to charge?"

She shook her head in wonder. "Jack..."

"Your first clue is when he takes out his credit card."

Jokes. He was telling elephant jokes. She gaped in astonishment.

"What did Tarzan say when he saw the elephant working in the coffee bar?"

He didn't wait for her to answer. Putting on a gruff voice, he said, "I didn't know the hippo had sold the place."

She laughed. She couldn't help it. She put her hand over her mouth to try to mask it, but she was laughing nonetheless.

"You smiling yet?" he asked her. "Or do I need to torture you some more?"

"I'm smiling," she admitted, and the laughter was still in her voice.

"Good," he said. "See you tomorrow."

"All right."

She hung up and stared at the telephone. His strategy had worked, she realized. There was a sense of warmth where a few moments before there had only been emptiness.

"He's just trying to charm me into doing things his way," she reminded herself out loud. But it didn't dim the warmth. Still smiling, she went to bed. She needed rest. Tomorrow she would be starting a new job, if there was any luck left in the world. And once she had that foundation of security, she would feel stronger. Maybe even strong enough to tell Jack Marin that he had to stay out of her life.

Chapter Four

"Oh Mikey, baby, please. Not now."

Wincing, Gayle gently patted the bulge where her baby was stretching his legs. She was sitting stiffly at the computer in a glass-enclosed room on the third floor of Earth Matters, Incorporated, trying to get a feel for the job Top Techs had sent her on. They hadn't given her much to go on, but the firm seemed to be involved in environmental impact research or something close to it. There were about twenty employees, including three software engineers and a pool of five secretaries. The rest were mainly scientists and lab workers. The building was beautifully landscaped and modern, of dark brick and tinted glass. The people she'd met so far were perfectly nice and friendly, and the entire situation seemed promising, but it was always a little nerve-wracking getting used to a new job.

Top Techs had called her first thing in the morning

and given her the information about this temporary opening, and she'd hurried over after a quick breakfast. Rio de Oro wasn't a very large town and there weren't likely to be too many temporary opportunities for the sort of work she did, so she had jumped at it. Phyllis Vernon, a warm older woman who was head of human resources for the company, had greeted her and showed her to the office she would be using.

"The boss wants to meet with you at ten-thirty. I'll show you to his office then." She glanced at her watch. "Can I get you anything? Do you have everything you need to get started?"

Gayle nodded. "I'll go over some of your most recent pamphlets to get a feel for what you value most in your work here—the sort of image you're trying to project. Then I can get some input from Mr...." She frowned, realizing she didn't know the boss's name, but Phyllis had already taken off in a new direction.

"The biggest thing on our agenda right now is the contract we're bidding on with TriTerraCorp. If we get that, we'll be secure for a good two years."

"TriTerraCorp?" Gayle said brightly. "I used to work there."

"No kidding? I hear they are a great place to work."

Gayle nodded. "They are. A lot of deadline pressure, but the people are great... So, what's he like?" she asked.

"The boss?" Phyllis shrugged, then grinned. "He's a sweetie. You'll like him." She started out the door, then had a thought and looked back in. "He may seem a little goofy at first. He's into elephant jokes this week. But if you can get beyond that, he's super. I'll come back to get you at ten-thirty and take you to meet the big guy.''

And she disappeared into the hallway.

Gayle sat very still, staring after her. Elephant jokes? No. It couldn't be.

But she knew right away that it was, and her heart started to thump loudly in her chest.

''Jack Marin.'' She said the name with involuntary acidity. Grabbing one of the company pamphlets, she flipped it open and searched the title page. There it was: Jack Marin, company president. ''Oh!''

She sat very still, a feeling of doom settling over her. She knew this was no coincidence. Jack had planned this and pulled it off at a few hours notice. He'd contacted the temp agency and set it up. He probably knew people there, just as he knew people at the fertility lab. And whom did she know? She bit her lip. No one much. Suddenly she felt very vulnerable.

She rose unsteadily, feeling slightly dizzy. She was going to leave before Jack found out she knew about his trap. Steadying herself, she took a deep breath and started for the lobby.

''Hey,'' said a voice from down the hall. ''Where do you think you're going?''

She didn't have to turn to know who it was, but she did anyway. She spun and glared at Jack as he came strolling toward her, looking very sure of himself.

''Home,'' she said defiantly as he came to a stop a few feet from her. But at the same time, she couldn't help but think that spurning him and his job would be much easier if he weren't so handsome, standing there in his crisp tan suit with a smile that reminded her of a certain cocky film star. She set her jaw and put more effort into it. "This won't work, Jack." Turning on her heel, she set off toward the glass doorway to the parking lot. "I need a real job," she called back over her shoulder.

He managed to beat her to the corner, blocking her way. "And I need a real Web designer. We're a perfect match."

She took another look at that devastating smile and suddenly felt paralyzed. "No," she said, shaking her head. "We're not. I'm not…" She looked toward the glass door, but it was no use. Her knees were buckling and her head was spinning.

"Gayle!"

He caught her in his arms before she fell, looking down into her face with real concern. She blinked up at him. The room was still slightly askew.

"Put me down," she said in a wavering voice that carried no conviction whatsoever, and he ignored her command, which wasn't surprising. The next thing she knew he was carrying her swiftly down the hall. She wanted to struggle and tell him to let her go, and she tried…but she was feeling so weak and it felt so very wonderful to be held. It was only seconds before she let her eyes drift shut and her head snuggle into his shoulder. He smelled of soap and sunshine, and she filled her lungs with it. She could feel the rounded muscles of his arms under his suit coat, and the hard panel of his chest beneath her cheek. A sense of his maleness washed over her, and she sighed softly. She felt warm and protected, and he felt strong and sure. It had been so very long since she'd felt so safe.

Before she knew it, he was gently laying her down on a small couch. She released him reluctantly, knowing she was going to have to open her eyes and get back to the real world.

"How do you feel?" he asked.

She looked up into his brown eyes, noticing there were golden flecks sparkling in the darkness of them, and then remembered that she was supposed to be trying to get away from this man. She took a deep breath, blinked, then began to try to sit up.

"No," he said firmly, pushing her back down. "You stay right where you are. I want to know what happened. Did you feel faint? Or dizzy? Does anything hurt?"

She frowned at him. This was ridiculous, really. She felt absolutely fine. "It was nothing. I'm okay. I didn't eat a very big breakfast before I came and I'm just a little weak, that's all."

He nodded, rising from the couch and walking across the room to slide into the chair behind a wide mahogany desk, where he picked up the telephone. "Betty, get me some food in here. Something nutritious. No, not coffee. A nice big glass of milk. Thanks." He frowned at Gayle, noticing that she'd sat up despite his orders, but he didn't say anything about it. The receiver was still to his ear.

"What's your obstetrician's number?" he asked, a pen poised to jot it down.

She sighed. "I'm fine. I don't need you to call my obstetrician."

He shrugged and calmly reached out to punch in a number. "Okay, I'll call mine."

"What?" At first she thought he was kidding, but he was obviously dialing. "What are you doing? You can't have an obstetrician!"

He raised one dark eyebrow. "Oh no? Why not?"

"Because..." Gayle shook her head, speechless. Wasn't it self evident?

He grinned at her, holding the receiver to his ear. "What are you, some kind of female chauvinist? Why can't I have an obstetrician?"

He was teasing her. She was sure of it. He hadn't really made a call. She relaxed. "Well, in the first place, the plumbing is all wrong for it," she pointed out.

He grinned. *"Vive la différence,"* he said with a wave of his hand. He was attempting to make the gesture look French, but it came across as more of a salute. For a moment, she had to fight to keep from laughing at him.

But suddenly he was talking into the receiver. "Jerry? Hi, it's me, Jack. Can I speak to the doc for a minute? Thanks."

Gayle began shaking her head. Darn it all, he hadn't been bluffing. "No," she said. "Jack, no...."

He held up a hand to stop her while he talked into the phone.

"Hi there. I've got a medical situation going on here. Yes. One of my, uh, employees is feeling woozy. She says she didn't eat much breakfast and thinks it's nothing serious, but I would really appreciate a second opinion on that." He paused, smirking at Gayle as she shook her head and gestured for him to stop. "Did I mention she is seven months pregnant? Okay. Thanks for the advice. Bye."

He put the receiver in its cradle. "She says to eat a good breakfast, take it easy and see if the food does the trick. Otherwise, I'm to bring you in to see her this afternoon." He grinned at her. "Dr. Vicky Richardson is one of my oldest friends. We grew up together. She'll be a big help to us from now on. You wait and see."

Gayle shook her head. "Do you ever listen to anyone else?" she asked him crisply. "Or is everything your call?"

He frowned. "I don't know why you can't appreciate the fact that I take an interest in your welfare," he said. "Some women would be flattered."

"You shouldn't have called her. I'm perfectly fine."

"Oh, sure. Perfectly healthy women faint at my feet every day. Hell, I'm used to it. No big deal." He dropped down to sit beside her on the couch and gave her a quizzical look. "But as I remember, you were running away from me at the time. You want to explain that?"

"That is self-explanatory. You tricked me into coming here today, and I'm not going to work for you."

"Why not?"

"Because you'll drive me crazy."

"No, I won't."

"Yes, you will. You'll watch everything I eat. You'll ask me if I had enough sleep last night. You'll follow me around with a sweater when the air conditioner is on."

He stared at her for a moment, as though she was making him see a side he hadn't acknowledged before, then chuckled in denial. "You really picture me as some sort of maiden aunt?" he asked. "That's not me. I won't bother you at all. Scout's honor."

She leaned away from him, needing more space. "You can't help but bother me," she said softly. Looking back at him, she added, "And you know it."

There was a question in his eyes, as if he weren't sure what she was referring to. But she wasn't really sure, either. So she quickly tried to manufacture an explanation. "I've got almost two months to go in my pregnancy. I can't spend all that time with you breathing down my neck. I can't work that way." As far as she was concerned, the matter was settled. "If you really need Web design, hire someone else."

His wide mouth twisted. "I do need some work done. I've been putting it off for much too long, because I didn't have a lead on anyone good to do the job." He sighed. "Gayle, like it or not, you're good. Top Techs faxed over your résumé along with some links to work you'd done. I took a look. I was very impressed. I'm surprised TriTerraCorp let you go."

"Like I said before, I was laid off." She hesitated. "After I left the company, I was going to develop a Web design consulting service, something I could do at home so that I would be able to stay with...the baby." She shrugged. "Then Hank died and my world turned upside down and I haven't had a chance to follow through on that. But I plan to—eventually."

"In the meantime, you need a temporary job."

She met his gaze. "I need a temporary *real* job. I don't need a charity position that puts me in line to be manipulated by you."

He frowned. She could tell he was beginning to get annoyed with her, and that was good. She could fight annoyance better than she could fight the sensual charm he usually employed.

Betty, Jack's secretary, arrived with a large glass of milk and a tray filled with bran breads and oatmeal muffins. Jack thanked the older woman and began doling out the food and drink as Betty left the room. Gayle took his offerings with a murmur of thanks, then began to relax a little, though she could tell he was watching every move she made.

"Are you going to try to monitor my daily intake of nutritious foods?" she asked him, sipping the deliciously cold milk and looking at him sideways as she did so. "I'm warning you right now, I'm not giving up my special vices. There are some things I just have to have."

"You don't smoke or drink alcohol, do you?" he asked, suddenly looking alarmed.

She gave him a sly look. "Worse," she teased.

He frowned. "Okay, give. What is it you just can't get enough of?"

She sighed as though it were a hard thing to admit to. "Chocolate," she said at last. "The creamy kind, with nuts and—"

"Chocolate." He sighed and then chuckled. "Well, moderation in all things, I always say. As long as you keep that in mind, I guess we can allow a little chocolate."

She carefully set down the glass, now half-empty,

and turned toward him with a determined glint in her eyes. "Listen, Jack. You can say whatever you like. In fact, you can live in any way that suits you. I don't care. I have no right to make rules for you." She set her jaw and poked him in the chest with her forefinger to emphasize her words as she added, "And you have no right to make rules for me. Even though I can tell that is exactly what you're planning. Which is exactly why I can't work for you."

He grabbed her hand and held it, ignoring the way she was tugging to get it back. "Gayle, you can live your life any way you choose. You're quite correct. I have no right to make rules for you." His gaze darkened. "But you can't deny me my son. I won't allow that."

She stopped tugging. He held her hand tightly, his fingers curled around hers as he pulled it up against his chest. He was staring so insistently into her eyes that she felt breathless. A flash of insight told her that he was going to get his way, no matter what she said or did. The only way she could avoid it was if she were to run away, disappear...and even then, he would probably find her. A wave of hopelessness swept over her.

"I'm not denying you..." Her voice faltered. Her mouth just wouldn't form the words—*your son*.

But he said, "Good," as though she'd said it, and his voice had a new, husky timber.

She looked up. He was still holding her hand against his chest, and he was going to kiss her. This time she was sure of it. She had to get away quickly, before he did. But for some reason she was frozen. She couldn't move.

His lips brushed hers once, twice, then again. She closed her eyes. If she didn't watch, maybe it wasn't really happening, and maybe that wasn't really a soft whimper coming from her own throat.

But he wasn't going to let her pretend. His tongue flickered against her lips and she accepted him with a sense of satisfaction, as though she'd been waiting for this for a long time. Her mind went blank, and for just a moment she was enveloped by sensations— the feel of his skin, the scent of his body heat, the sound of the passion rising in his throat, the hot, sweet taste of his mouth on hers.

And then it was over.

"I didn't mean to do that," he told her gruffly, drawing back.

"Neither did I," she said softly, looking away and trying to pretend she wasn't dealing with a heartbeat that threatened to drown out their voices.

"I mean it," he said, looking angry with himself and turning away. "We can't let things like that cloud the situation."

Reaching out for her milk, Gayle willed her hand not to shake as she grasped the glass and took a last long sip before she set it back down.

"Feeling better?" he asked a few moments later.

"Yes—much."

There was genuine relief in his face. It stopped her cold. She was speechless. He really seemed to care. A feeling washed over her, a feeling warmer than his kiss had been. It felt so good to have someone care. She realized she must be lonelier than she'd thought, and for just a second, she had the urge to walk into his arms.

But she stopped herself in time, slapped in the face by a dose of reality. It was Mikey he cared about. She had to remember that. As Jack went on, talking about how good it was going to be to have her working so close by, she tried to conceal her conflicting emotions. Working here was going to be a constant roller coaster if she didn't watch out.

Still, when she tried to conjure up her remaining sense of outrage, she found the fight had drained out of her, and as he went on, telling her how much he really needed a Web presence for his company, how very important it was that she be the one who designed it, how the very future of his firm depended on this all going well, she realized she had let him put her into the position of doing exactly what he wanted once again.

That was a very bad habit to get into. If she was going to work for him, she was going to have to find a way to avoid doing that again. But even more important, she was going to have to find a way to avoid feeling this deep attraction every time she looked at him. Because, kisses or no, she knew very well it wasn't really a two-way street. He might give her suggestive looks, but there was always an impression of detachment about him. He didn't want to get close anymore than she did. Maybe that would be their saving grace.

Jack sat at his desk staring out the huge bay window at the pine-covered hill as the light began to fade into evening. He was restless, filled with a vague sense of unease. And he shouldn't be. He wasn't sure why he didn't feel more pleased.

He had what he wanted, didn't he? Gayle was staying on and working where he could both keep an eye on her and make sure she had everything she needed. And he had almost two months to use all his powers of persuasion to get her to see the wisdom of giving him custody of the baby.

Well, that was the irony, wasn't it? Because the better he got to know Gayle, the harder it became to imagine her giving up her baby.

It had seemed so simple at first. When he'd realized what the situation was, he'd assumed she'd be a pushover for the proposition. A young widow without a job or a secure base in the community—what was she going to do? Once she'd looked at the problem realistically and weighed all he had to offer, she would sadly but wisely agree his plan was best for them all.

Anyway, that had been the scenario he'd dreamed up. Now he knew that would never happen, not that easily. He was going to have to think of a way to make her see that letting him raise his son was the right thing to do. Given the time he had, he would surely think of something.

But he shouldn't have kissed her. Talk about muddying the waters. Damn! That had been a stupid thing to do. Stupid, but certainly predictable. She was just so kissable, and it had come so naturally. She was so soft and warm and her mouth had tasted like—

No! He slapped the flat of his hand down on the desk. He wasn't going to think about that. And he had to be more careful in the future. After all, he was the one with the agenda. He wanted his son and he definitely did not want a woman to go with the package. When he'd made up his mind to take this path, he'd made a pledge to himself—no women. His next eighteen years were going to be devoted to raising his son. No complications allowed.

"Just me and Mikey," he muttered under his breath, and grinned as he wrapped his thoughts around the prospect. He'd planned to name his son Anthony, after his father. He knew the old man would like that. But Michael wasn't so bad. Maybe Michael Anthony.

"Anthony Michael," he whispered. Yeah, that sounded good. He could picture the boy: reddish hair, freckles on his nose, an impish look. His son. His heart swelled with an emotion that almost choked him. He had his son. This time, he wasn't going to lose him.

Chapter Five

Of course, the situation was impossible. Gayle had known it would be. And the longer she stayed, the worse it got. She was aware of Jack, and his claim on her life, every minute of the day. And it wasn't really even his fault. He went out of his way to keep a low profile around her. He didn't do anything disturbing—not outright. He came in with a friendly smile in the morning, but he didn't linger at her desk. He looked up when she passed his open office door and gave her a nod, maybe a smile, but he didn't ever encourage a chat. And he never tried to eat lunch with her, or see her after hours. When he wanted information from her or wanted to convey an idea, he sent in Betty as liaison. All in all, he was being true to his word.

But it didn't make any difference. The fact that he was there was enough to throw her off. The fact that she was breathing the same air as a practical stranger who had—or thought he had—a claim on her baby, was enough. It made her crazy.

Add to that the memory of his kiss. She tried to forget it, but that wasn't possible. Every time she passed him in the hall, she found herself glancing at his mouth, and then she would have to look away quickly and pray he hadn't noticed. It was humiliating. She felt like an adolescent again, obsessed with whether the boy she had a crush on liked her or not. She had to be careful or she might find herself doodling intertwining initials on her work—decorated with little hearts.

And finally, the fact that all the other women in the office wanted to talk about him all the time didn't help. Gayle couldn't get them away from the subject. They discussed his attire and tried to divine his mood, and gossiped about his love life. She tried to stay out of it, but day after day she was drawn in. It seemed he was the favorite topic of conversation, as though everyone's life revolved around the man.

"Did you see the tie Mr. Marin has on today?" one of the female geologists asked her one noon as she sat around the table in the lunch room with a group of the women. "It's so cute. It's got little elephants running all over it."

"Elephants!" Gayle exclaimed, surprised to hear about pachyderms once again. "What is it with this man and elephants?"

"Listen," Betty, his secretary told her, leaning across the table with a knowing look. "Be glad he's into elephants these days. Last year it was knock-knock jokes, and we were all going demented with the silly puns."

"Oh, I loved the knock-knock jokes," Phyllis countered as she polished off a raspberry yogurt. "I think I told him as many as he told me." She looked smug. "My son Tommy was constantly giving me new ones he'd heard at school." Her green eyes took on a wistful air. "Mr. Marin went with Tommy to his Boy Scout troop's Daddy and Me night last month. Tommy was so proud to have a man like that to show off."

Gayle nodded sympathetically, knowing that Phyllis was a widow, too. It was certainly nice of Jack to do a thing like that, but to tell the truth, she didn't want to hear about it. Glancing around the table, she couldn't help but wish someone would tell her something bad about the man. What the heck? There had to be something. But no one did.

Unfortunately, he was about the most attractive man she'd ever known. That didn't make anything any easier.

And she had to contend with his attractiveness once again at the beginning of the next week. She'd been congratulating herself on having made it through an entire weekend without one call—much less a visit—from Jack when he appeared in the doorway of her office. She caught her breath in her throat as she looked at him.

"Good morning," he said, though his eyes weren't friendly. "Mind if I interrupt you for a moment?"

"No, of course not," she said quickly, wishing her heart wouldn't speed up as though she'd just had a narrow escape from death. "Come on in."

He moves like a jungle cat, she thought to herself as took a seat on the other side of her desk. *And meanwhile, I'm more like a tugboat.*

But thinking like that wasn't going to help anything, so she made herself shelve it for the time being. It was obvious he had something serious to discuss.

"I had a phone call from the fertility lab today," he said, watching her reaction. "I hear you've been requesting documentation that proves my claim to be the baby's father."

She flushed. "Do you have a problem with my request?" she asked stiffly.

"No," he said slowly, though his eyes were contradicting the statement. "You can request all the paperwork and proof that you want. That's your right." His eyes darkened. "But why did you make an appointment with a lawyer?"

Her cheeks were rosier than ever, but she held her head high. "What? Did the lawyer call you, too?"

"No."

"Then how do you know I saw a lawyer?"

He shrugged carelessly. "I have my sources."

Sure. The lawyer's secretary probably called him daily with updates on who was coming and who was going. Why did it seem as though everyone in town was on his side? For a moment, resentment quivered inside her, but she knew self-pity was only going to weaken her position, so she forced it down again.

"Okay, Boss," she said coolly, sitting back in her chair. "Here's the lowdown on my life. Very recently, I was calmly going along, preparing to have my baby, when all of a sudden, a stranger swooped in and wrecked all my plans, telling me he had a right to half of my most precious possession. Did you think I was going to just nod and say, 'Sure, whatever you say,' without checking on the facts of the matter? Without consulting a lawyer to see what my rights are? What my obligations and liabilities are?''

"Of course not," he said dismissively. "I would expect you to do exactly that." He leaned closer, holding her gaze with the intensity of his own. "Just a word of warning, though. Don't try to get a court order barring me from having equal access to my son. I think it's safe to say I can probably afford more expensive lawyers than you can."

She sat there, speechless. What exactly was he threatening her with?

"You know," he continued, though his tone had lightened considerably and the coldness seemed to be melting from his expression, "it would make it so much easier on everyone if you would just do what's best for Mikey."

She stared at him. He was absolutely serious. He really thought that she would have to agree—if she really thought things through—that Mikey would have a better life with him than he possibly could with her. The arrogance of the man! The conceit! It should have made her furious, but to her own surprise, it was so over the top, it only made her want to laugh.

"Jack," she said, shaking her head and holding back the laughter that was trying to bubble up her throat, "You're impossible. You may be richer than I am. You may be able to hire expensive lawyers. You may be able to hire tutors and afford tuition at swanky private schools. But you'll never be able to be what I can be to my son. You'll never be his mother.''

A light seemed to dim in his eyes. "And you'll never be his father," he reminded her.

The laughter died, because he was right. But so was she. They were at a stalemate. What were they going to do?

Stall for time, she told herself. *Time and knowledge may be all you will have to counter his money and connections.* And under those circumstances, the more she knew, the better. Which reminded her.

"You still haven't told me why you are so anxious to have a son," she said.

He looked at her coolly, but searching deep into his eyes, she could have sworn there was something grave and tragic going on there.

"I had a very bad marriage," he told her quietly. "And so did my parents. I'm not going to risk something like that again. And at the same time, I'm human. I want..." He caught himself, shaking his head. "No, let me put it another way. I *need* to produce something lasting. I need to fill a profound loneliness in my soul, and in my family. I need a son." His mouth twisted in a crooked smile that purposefully took some of the emotion out of his very private words. "Is that good enough for you?"

Whether it was or not, he didn't really seem to care. He'd released his salvo of weapons and he was ready to go, rising and turning toward the door.

"Wait," she said, pushing back her auburn hair with a hand that she hoped wasn't shaking. "Tell me one more thing. How did you know about the mix-up at the lab? Why did you know before they told me?''

He stared down at her, wondering how much he really wanted her to know. In fact, he'd just as soon she knew nothing. But if he told her how it had really been, maybe she would see how committed he was to this enterprise. Maybe she would understand that he wasn't going to give up easily. Slowly, he sat back down again.

''Okay,'' he said. ''Here's the way it was. About a year ago, I was on automatic pilot, going through the motions of life. My marriage had failed. My family was unhappy with me. There didn't seem to be much point to it all, any purpose. Then, little by little, a thought grew in me, a brilliant idea.''

He paused, remembering. The idea of having a surrogate produce a child for him had been in the back of his mind for a long time, ever since his wife had dashed his hopes and walked out on him, taking his dream of a houseful of children with her. He knew he would never marry again, and he'd faced a life without the family he'd always wanted, without children to carry on the family name. He wanted a son, needed him desperately, with every fiber of his being. And eventually, he'd done something about it.

He resumed his story. ''I looked into surrogate mothering and found it really was possible. I brought it up with my family—and after they got over the initial shock, they started to get excited, too. It changed everything. It brightened our lives, restored hope in the future, gave us all something to live for. And when the lab told me my baby had been conceived…'' His voice choked slightly and he cleared his throat.

He looked at Gayle, trying to judge if he was getting through to her or not. There was so much more he could tell her, but he didn't want to overdo it. He didn't think he needed to tell her about all the rigmarole he'd gone through, the consultations and the psychological profiling and the counseling sessions.

Gayle was obviously waiting to hear the rest. He drew in a deep breath. ''About a month ago, they told me the surrogate mother had miscarried.''

Gayle bit her lip, but didn't say anything. She could imagine how she would have felt at such news.

''I was devastated,'' he said simply. ''I felt like I had to see the mother of my baby, to share my grief with what I was sure had to be her own. I wanted to know all the details. I wanted to take care of her. I tried to find her, but they wouldn't let me know who she was. They said it was against regulations.'' He gazed at Gayle levelly. ''So I went to a judge who is a friend of my father's and I got a court order.''

She gulped. There it was again—his connections, his ability to get things done. She knew all that could be turned against her if need be.

''That's when it all came out. When I took in an expert to look over the data, he found that a lab technician had made a mistake and had been covering it up. Even the lab didn't know. But my baby hadn't died at all. My baby was still very much alive, and growing healthily, just inside a different mother. You.''

Her blue eyes widened. ''So you were the one who told the lab.''

He nodded. "That's why I knew before you did. And why I knew who you were."

She took a deep breath. If he hadn't done the audit, no one would have known.

"Anyway, now you know," he said. Rising, he lingered for just a moment, as though he couldn't stop looking at her. Reaching down, he cupped her warm cheek with his hand and smiled into her eyes.

"There is one other thing that can't be denied," he said softly. "I couldn't have given my son a more beautiful mother if I'd tried."

The anxiety she'd been feeling evaporated. He scared her, annoyed her, infuriated her, and yet his touch pushed all that aside as the desire to be kissed again surged in her chest, an urgent impulse that seemed capable of overpowering all rational thought and rendering her helpless. She was drawn to him, like a moth to the flame. She wanted to feel his lips on hers.

But there wasn't time for that. Without warning, the office door flew open and two of the younger lab technicians stood in the doorway staring at the two of them, mouths agape.

Jack dropped his hand and turned, smiled at the women and nodded as he slipped past them and out into the corridor. "Good morning, ladies," he said as he went. "Great day, isn't it?"

They muttered something inarticulate, but their gazes were on Gayle, who had to pretend nothing had happened, while remaining cheerful and keeping her head together. It wasn't easy. Her mind was full of recriminations and regrets. Had he seen the desire in her eyes? Had she made it so obvious that anyone could sense it? Why was she so weak when he came close? It wasn't like her and she didn't like it. Jack had stirred the pot again.

He upset her—and made her curious to know more about him. She hadn't really delved into his marriage in any meaningful way. Thinking back, she couldn't remember exactly how he'd acted when talking about his marriage the day they'd met. Her mind had been on other things at the time. But finding out what his wife had been like, and why they had split up, would be very helpful in filling in the picture somewhat. Maybe it was time to see what she could learn about the ex-Mrs. Marin.

Luckily, Gayle knew someone who could help her, and she didn't think this source would make a clandestine telephone call to Jack as soon as she was through talking to her. Kate Marker was the information librarian at the local library, and Gayle had been friends with her ever since moving to Rio de Oro. A discreet request for a search of the local newspaper's archive files yielded a nice little folder of photocopies of the records on microfiche for her to peruse privately that evening when she got home from work. She made herself a pot of tea, put her feet up and began going through them as soon as she got in. Eventually, she found the engagement announcement notice with a picture of Jack and his fiancée, both looking very young and very happy. The bride-to-be's name had been Kiki Vanderhaven before she'd married Jack, and she was as beautiful as a supermodel, tall and sleek and sophisticated, with almond-shaped eyes and lustrous brown hair. The copy said she was from Chicago, but had graduated from UCLA with Jack. It looked like their wedding had taken place shortly after graduation.

"Well, now you know," Gayle told herself wryly. A small, hard lump had settled in the pit of her stomach and she didn't let herself wonder why.

The remaining clips listed Jack's professional and public service pursuits as well as charity functions Kiki quickly became involved in. For a period of two or three years, she seemed to be in a constant social whirl. Then suddenly, she was gone, and the only notations were of Jack alone. There was no notice of any divorce, though that might not be unusual. She was just…gone.

Gayle sighed and put the papers back in the folder to return to her librarian friend. Now she wished she hadn't looked at them. It felt sort of like eavesdropping. Did she know any more than she'd known before? Not really. The only thing she was sure of was that Jack's wife had been a real beauty, but Gayle would have expected that, anyway.

Mikey kicked and she put a hand over his foot and hummed softly to him. In just a few weeks, the child would be in her arms. Was Jack going to be her constant shadow, waiting to grab her baby every time she put him down? She shuddered, thinking about it. Still, she couldn't get his face out of her thoughts. He was becoming too much a part of her life, whether she liked it or not.

Chapter Six

Jack glanced at the clock set above the stainless steel oven in his condominium kitchen. Six-forty. Gayle was late. He frowned, drumming his fingers on the black marble countertop. He should have insisted on picking her up and bringing her over himself. What if she stood him up?

But she wouldn't do that. Not without calling, anyway.

He turned restlessly and looked at his place, trying to see it with her eyes. It was quiet. Too quiet? Should he put on some music, maybe something classy…Chopin? But he listened again and heard the rumble of the surf below his balcony, the call of gulls from the pier, the shout of one surfer to another, and he decided to leave well enough alone. This was home and he liked it.

He did a quick survey of the preparations he'd made. Marta, the woman who came by and did his cleaning twice a week, had set the table for him, and he had to say she'd done a darn good job. The green tablecloth looked crisp and fresh, a perfect setting for the small arrangement of tiny yellow daffodils he'd brought home and put into a vase for the center of the table. The pale green plates and graceful sterling flatware looked perfect with the bright yellow napkins. Rays from the setting sun shot through the beveled glass of his windows, touching the crystal wine goblets and sending sparks shimmering around the room, like diamonds. The effect was spectacular. She was going to like that.

The only problem was, if she didn't get here soon, the sun would set and the effect would be gone. Where the hell was she?

He moved aimlessly through the room, ending up at the French doors leading out onto the balcony that overlooked the ocean. Shoving his hands deep into his pockets, he frowned at the peaceful scene spread out before him, not seeing it at all as he mulled over the situation. Maybe she'd changed her mind and decided not to come, after all. She'd hesitated when he'd invited her to dinner at his place. She'd wanted to turn him down. He'd seen it in her eyes as soon as he'd brought it up. In fact, she wanted to find a way to push him out of her life for good. He knew that. But that wasn't going to happen. He was going to have to make her face that.

He heard her at the door and he smiled with relief. She'd come. Good. Tonight he was going to show her how serious he was about his son. The atmosphere around the office had made it very hard to bring the subject up again, especially after their brief

encounter in her office the other day. That was why
he'd asked her here. He was ready to lay down the
law. After tonight, she would know how it was going
to have to be. It was time to set some guidelines and
prepare for the future. He walked toward the door
with a spring in his step and a sense of confidence
in the outcome.

The door opened, and there he was—all six foot
of stunningly handsome man. Every nerve ending
Gayle possessed quivered with awareness and her
heart sank. This was going to be tough. Real tough.
And she wasn't even sure she was going to be able
to do it.

She shouldn't have come. When was she going to
learn to follow her instincts? She'd known it would
be a mistake to come to his condo and have dinner
with him. Why hadn't she told him to keep his
charming ways in storage until she could figure out
a plan to disentangle herself from this sticky situation?

He came close, reaching to help her remove her
jacket, and his hand brushed her neck. She gasped
softly, drawing away from him and then regretting
her own involuntary reaction. But her skin still tin-
gled. She reached up to rub the spot, trying to make
it stop, but her gaze met his and she could see that
he knew exactly what was going on. Quickly, she
dropped her hand and turned away.

"You have a lovely home," she stated a bit formally as she walked into the middle of the living
room. But she meant what she said. The place was
spacious and beautiful, and at first glance, it certainly

appeared to have been designed with taste and intelligence. Everything looked expensive and well maintained. "Very impressive."

"Thank you. *I* like it." He hung her jacket on a wrought-iron hook in the entry hall and followed her into the room.

"Did you...have you lived here long?"

He threw her a knowing glance. "If what you mean is did I live here when I was married, the answer is yes."

She flushed, embarrassed that he'd seen through her so easily. Turning, she took another look around the room, hunting for evidence of a feminine touch. She didn't find any. A display case filled with huge and beautiful mineral specimens sat at one side of the room, and a bookcase filled with well-used books and various angular sculptures stood across from it. The three main pictures that hung on the papered walls were enhanced depictions of World War II fighter planes. The furniture was Danish wood, but didn't look as though it might have been picked out by a woman named Kiki. Gayle wondered fleetingly if that had been part of the problem. Did Jack overwhelm the relationship? Did everything always have to be his way?

"How long ago was your divorce?" she asked.

A storm swept into his gaze and she knew right away she was treading on forbidden ground. Well, tough. He thought he could turn her life upside down and then withhold his own life story at will. Well, he was going to have to think again. She stared at him, daring him to tell her the truth.

"Over five years ago," he said shortly. "But my

dead marriage is not an issue we need to get into. I didn't ask you here for that."

"I see," she said archly, giving him a sideways glance as she turned to look through the glass doors leading out onto the balcony. "So you *did* have an agenda when you invited me. And here I thought you just wanted to feed me so you could make sure I was eating something you approved of." She glanced toward the kitchen. "Something does smell awfully good."

"Macadamia encrusted salmon, baby asparagus, buttered fettuccine and green salad with raspberry vinaigrette dressing," he offered by way of explanation.

Her eyes widened with appreciation. "So you cook, too," she murmured.

His eyes met hers and a sudden crooked grin softened his handsome face. "I've got many talents we haven't had a chance to explore," he noted calmly. "All in good time."

Their eyes met and she could have sworn sparks flew, but then she realized it must have been the evening sunlight slanting in through the crystal wine goblets on his table, and she breathed a tiny sigh of relief.

He seemed to feel the same way, because he turned and reached for the goblets. "We'll eat in a few minutes," he told her. "Let me pour you a drink in the meantime."

"Oh no," she said, startled. "No alcohol."

"Sparkling cider," he said reassuringly as he reached for a green bottle that was waiting on the black marble countertop, and poured the golden liquid into the glasses. "No alcohol in it at all."

"Just pretend," she murmured, taking the glass he offered her. The words echoed in her mind, confusing her a little. What was it they were pretending, actually?

"To Mikey," he said, raising his glass to clink with hers.

"To Mikey," she repeated, then took a sip. The liquid felt cool and soothing as it went down, and she resisted the impulse to drain her glass. Reluctantly, she had to admit to herself that it was considerate of him to drink cider, too, to keep her company. The well-stocked wine rack at the entrance to the kitchen gave evidence that he was not a teetotaler. *Okay,* she told herself. *Score one point in his favor. But don't let it undermine your determination!*

"Why don't you sit down?" he suggested, pulling out a chair for her at the table. "I'll get dinner on."

"Oh. Don't you, uh, want me to help?"

"No." He smiled at her. "I want you to relax. Sit down and let yourself be pampered for a little while."

He brought out the food and served it with a deft attention to style that made her marvel. Then he joined her, refilled their glasses with cider, and they began to eat.

It was wonderful. She almost resented how good everything was. The salmon seemed to melt in her mouth. The macadamia crust was buttery and light. The salad was heavenly. The fettuccine was a perfect foil. Every bite made her want to sigh with happiness. She glanced at him and knew he was monitoring her reaction, and pretty darn pleased with what he saw. There was more than one sort of seduction, and she knew very well he was trying hard to seduce her—not into anything romantic, but into letting him have his way with her in other directions. She also knew she was much more susceptible to falling into his trap than she would have liked to admit.

She had to stay strong. It was time for her to launch into the speech she'd been preparing to deliver for days now. It was time for her to set him straight and let him see that she could be as tough as he could—as tough as she had to be to defend her child.

And Mikey was going to be *her* child. Not their child. Gayle was going to decide what to do about him and what he needed in life. She understood that Jack could press his legal perquisites to gain access. But if he was going to do that she was not going to roll over and play dead. No matter what, she was going to do what was in the best interest of her child. Even if Jack didn't like it.

At least that was the theory. The speech had seemed quite effective when delivered to her bathroom mirror. She was planning to say, "Enough is enough," and very firmly, too. She thought the words. She set her jaw. She took a deep breath. Her lips moved.

But what she actually said was, "Oh, this is so delicious."

His smile seemed pleased. "More cider?"

She shook her head. "I'd better not. My head is spinning as it is."

His eyes were smiling now. "Ah yes. I can see that cider affects you pretty dramatically."

Funny, but it really did seem more like champagne than cider. She laughed. "What is it about bubbles that makes everything seem lighter?"

"Effervescence. Kind of like you."

She looked at him in surprise. "You find me effervescent?"

He put his head to the side, considering. "Yes, I think I do. I've noticed you're the kind of woman who lights up a room when she comes into it."

Oh boy. Now that was heavy artillery. She almost giggled. She couldn't help but blossom under his flattery, even as she warned herself not to listen to him. "What a nice thing to say," she murmured.

"It's the truth." Suddenly his eyes changed. He put down his glass and pushed back his chair. "If you're finished, there is something I want to show you," he said.

She looked at him, suddenly wary. "What is it?"

"You'll see."

She frowned, not sure she was in the mood for surprises. But she let him help her up and lead her across the living room toward a hallway.

"I want you to see the room I've prepared for the baby," he said. He stopped in front of a closed door and looked down into her face, his eyes earnest. " I just want you to understand how committed I am to this fatherhood thing. Come on in here and take a look."

She'd been afraid she wasn't going to like his version of show-and-tell, and now she knew for sure. But what had she expected? He was always working toward his goal. And so was she. Dreading what she was going to see, she walked in through the door he opened for her.

And what she saw was astonishing—the most beautiful baby's room she'd ever seen. A huge, hand-painted mural of Noah's ark filled one wall, with the boat riding on a rainbow and the animals, including elephants, coming off two by two. The motif was echoed in the curtains, the bedding in the antique wooden crib and even on the changing-table pad. Stacks of baby clothes were folded neatly on the dresser. He even had a full set of Childhood Charmers rompers—a very expensive clothing line she loved—sitting on a shelf, and she could have sworn the company had gone out of business. The rocking horse in the corner was actually a rocking elephant, and a choo-choo train large enough for a toddler to ride in sat waiting at the other end of the room. The setting was poised, ready, almost breathless with anticipation. All it needed was a child.

She turned slowly, then went to the changing table and picked up a little blue shirt, slipping her hand into it. It was so tiny it made her heart ache. This big man had prepared for a tiny little baby as though it were a real labor of love. He wanted a baby so badly—yearned desperately for a little one. There was no denying it.

She was touched for a moment, deeply touched almost to the point of becoming teary, and then she hardened her heart, pulling her hand out of the little shirt and dropping it on the table. She stepped back. What was she thinking? Surely no man would have gone out and bought all these things on his own.

How would he have known what to buy? Something didn't seem right here.

She couldn't help but wonder if perhaps this room *hadn't* just been set up in the last few weeks. Could those baby things have been put in place years ago...for a different child? Maybe even a child he'd had with his ex-wife?

"What did you do, have some expensive designer come in to decorate and stock the room for you?" she asked evenly, turning to challenge him.

He blinked, as though surprised by her tone. "No." He gave her a lopsided smile, looking almost shy. "Actually, Vicky, my obstetrician friend, helped me. She's good with baby things."

"Oh." She'd had a few conversations with Vicky and liked her a lot. His explanation swept away Gayle's objections and left her raw and vulnerable to the obvious nature of his need for this child. Now obviously wasn't the time to try to dig into his past. She looked around again, noted the tiny blue booties sitting in wait on the dresser, the Babar sleeping jumper, the diaper pins decorated with little elephant heads. His soul was laid open for her in this room. He wanted this baby—her baby—more than he wanted anything else. The room sang with his love. No matter what else happened between them, she had to acknowledge that.

She wished she didn't have to. She wished she could turn away and leave him and never look back. But she knew something was happening here, something that was going to make it even harder to get out of this situation.

She turned and looked at him. "I had a speech

ready to give you when I came tonight," she said simply.

"Did you?"

"Yes." She reached up and pushed her hair back. "All about how impossible this was. How I thought it would be best if I moved out of town, got away from you."

His eyes darkened. "Where were you planning to go?"

She sighed and shrugged lightly. "A friend of mine suggested Liechtenstein."

"That's a long commute."

Gazing into his eyes, she was utterly candid. "I really had convinced myself that it would be best to get away from you and your influence on this child."

He winced, as though she'd found a weakness in his defenses—a weakness that had to be fortified. "Gayle, don't you understand?" he said softly, his eyes burning into hers. "You can't get away from my influence on that child. My influence has been planted inside you. It's taken root."

She gasped, outraged. "Oh, for heaven's sake! What a thing to say."

He shrugged. "A little crude, perhaps. But it carries the meaning I want to convey." He stepped closer, touching her arm and adding softly, "You can run, but you can't hide. You can't shake off my influence. There's nothing you can do about that. It's done."

She felt the import of his words, but, still she lifted her chin and fought back. "And at the same time, you can't get away from mine. This is my baby." She placed her hands over her stomach. "After I've carried him for nine months, you can't possibly imagine I would ever give him up.''

He was silent for a long moment, then he looked at her with such intensity, she almost gasped again. ''Women give up babies for adoption all the time.''

She shook her head, feeling sad but strong in this. ''Not me. Not this baby. Never.''

She searched his eyes, expecting anger, but there was no evidence of any. Instead, she thought she saw a strange acceptance, as though he'd come to some sort of realization about this situation. But she could be wrong. Maybe he just didn't believe she was serious. Maybe he still thought he could convince her to change her mind.

At any rate, his gaze lightened and he seemed content to drop the subject for the time being. Leading her back into the living room, he chatted about inconsequential things, and she gradually lost the defensive posture that had been created by their argument. Soon she was chatting back, enjoying him. He was a very engaging man. They ate the delicious dessert he'd concocted—raspberries with vanilla cream—and then they walked out onto the balcony to look at the surf in the moonlight.

Gayle felt good again. As long as they stayed off the subject of her baby, they seemed to get along marvelously. She looked out at the soft purple darkness, at the silver moon riding high in the sky, at the lacy foam as the water lapped the shore, and she sighed.

''I used to dream of being in a place just like this when I was growing up in Alaska,'' she told him, turning to look up at him as he leaned against the railing beside her. "I would close my eyes and picture a beach with white sand and blue-green water, and I would dance...." She laughed softly as she let the memory float away. "And then I would open my eyes and look out at the endless white snow and shiver."

"You won't shiver tonight," he said lightly, letting his fingers trail against her neck as he pushed back a stray lock of her hair. "It's very warm. It feels like there's a Santa Ana blowing."

She nodded, feeling a different sort of shivering and trying not to show it. "I wonder if the sand is still warm from being in the sun all day," she murmured.

"There's one way to find out," he said, taking her arm. "Let's go down and walk barefoot in it."

"Oh, do you think we should?"

"No," he told her, his grin seductively mischievous. "But we'll do it anyway."

The sand *was* still warm and her feet sank down into it, making her laugh. They went to the edge of the water and played tag with the waves that rippled up along the shoreline. He teased her and she teased him. She almost forgot she was pregnant as they made their way toward the pier. She wasn't exactly dancing, but he made her feel as though she were.

Suddenly, she was out of breath and so tired she thought she would collapse if she took another step. Jack scooped her up in his arms and carried her over to where a palm tree bent so low to the ground it formed a perfect backrest. He set her gently on the sand, then dropped to sit beside her.

"Oh, Mikey, please don't," she said, half laughing as she rubbed her belly. "He wants to get out and run, too, only he's doing it inside, and it's getting a bit painful."

Jack was silent for a minute, then reached out his hand. "May I?" he asked, his hand suspended a few inches away from her body.

She looked at him, bemused. "Sure. Go ahead."

And then she caught her breath as he touched her. His hand slipped lightly over the hard, rounded swell, then stopped as he felt a little leg bulge out. He looked at Gayle, his eyes wide. Even in the darkness, she could see his enchantment. The bulge moved and his hand followed. Their gazes met and they laughed together.

"Oh my God," he breathed with real wonder in his voice. "It's such a miracle. It's a magic thing, to think that he's in there. So near and yet so far."

She nodded. His hand was still on her baby. He was so close, she could breathe his scent, and it was provocatively masculine, wrapping around her like a protective cloak. He was looking down at her.

"Moonlight becomes you," he said softly. "You look like a sea princess."

"Oh, Jack," she said, shaking her head, feeling pitiful. "I wish you would quit saying things like that."

"That you're beautiful?"

She hesitated. "Yes, things like that."

His free hand was brushing hair back out of her eyes. "Why? Does it embarrass you?"

"No, it's just that…well, I don't feel very beautiful right now."

His hand was lingering against her skin, creating

a tingling wherever the fingers touched. "Well, I have to admit," he said softly, "I'm not exactly ecstatic about it, either."

Her mind was getting groggy, intoxicated by his touch. She couldn't quite understand what he was getting at. "What do you mean?"

"You being so beautiful." His finger traced her lower lip. "It makes you that much harder to resist."

She wanted to nuzzle into the palm of his hand, to arch into his arms. Somehow his words weren't making much sense, but his body language said it all. She wanted to be kissed again. She yearned for it, and as she turned her face up to his, she knew he would see it in her eyes.

"I'm not something you're supposed to resist," she murmured. "I...I mean—"

"Good," he said decisively. "Because I'm sick of trying."

She'd been aching for his kiss ever since that first day he'd carried her into his office. She'd dreamed about it at night, and her thoughts had lingered on the sensations of it all through the day.

But memories weren't as good as the real thing. His lips touched hers and she sighed with happiness as she responded. His warmth filled her and she felt as though a tension had been released inside her. This was what she needed, more than water, more than air. She turned toward him, hungry for more contact, and he pulled her into his arms, folding her into his embrace. Nothing penetrated the perfect union they made, twined together, drinking heat from each other's lips.

She'd never known kisses could be like this, so

delicious, so hypnotic. She didn't want it ever to end, and she pushed all thought away, knowing too much realism would spoil the magic. She was drifting on a sea of sensation and she'd never been so completely enchanted before.

Finally he lifted his lips from hers, but only to chuckle low in his throat and tell her softly, "I can't stop. You're like peanuts."

She blinked like a deep-sea diver coming up for air. "Peanuts? What are you talking about?"

He dropped a kiss on her lips. "You're irresistible."

"Oh." She relaxed and smiled. "Like potato chips?"

"Better." He kissed her again. "Like Bing cherries at peak season."

"Or Strauss waltzes."

"Or golden retriever puppies."

They laughed together, and then his mouth claimed hers again and she abandoned herself to the joy of it.

Until she realized what this could lead to. Her own body brought the subject up by reacting in ways she hadn't expected. The thought of giving in to her desire skimmed into her consciousness and she frowned, trying to force it away. She didn't want to think about making love. But there it was, taunting her. She opened her eyes and looked at the man beside her. What was wrong with her? How could she be sitting here making out like a teenager on a beach? And how could she think about sex at a time like this? Here she was, going on eight months pregnant. Why would she do such a thing?

Because you're human, the sensible side of her brain told her serenely. *Because you're a woman who's been without a man for much too long...like just about forever. Because you're kissing the most attractive man you've ever known. It's only natural.*

Only natural—and a giant wet blanket on her fun. She knew it was time to cut this off. If *she* was thinking about making love, she knew darn well he'd been thinking about it, too. She drew back slowly, taking last, fleeting kisses and then stopping with reluctance.

He looked down at her with eyes that seemed to hint at the sort of romance she'd never known, and she sighed, shaking her head and smiling at him.

"This isn't going to work, you know," she said sadly.

His handsome face took on just the slightest scowl. "Isn't it?"

"No." She pulled away entirely and began straightening her clothing. "I'm not going to change my mind."

He was silent for a long moment, looking out to sea. "What *would* change your mind?" he asked her at last.

"Nothing," she said quickly, then began to try to pull herself up.

He rose and reached out to help her. "Something is going to have to," he said evenly. "I'm not going to try to snow you about this, Gayle. My objective hasn't changed. And it won't."

"Your objective and my objective hit an impasse somewhere between 'might have' and 'never,

ever.'" She squared her shoulders. "So now listen to me, because I'm ready to say my piece."

She faced him and finally put her prepared speech to use, marshaling her arguments with a sort of forlorn hope, bombarding him with facts, letting him know sharing custody would be no picnic.

"I won't make it easy for you," she warned him. "Why should I? I didn't ask for this to happen."

They began to walk back toward his condo and she went on, piling up the declarations of intent, letting him have it. Beyond anything else, he had to understand that this was not going to be a good thing to do. He would be much happier and more satisfied if he gave up and found himself a new mother for a new baby that could be all his. He might have "planted his influence" inside her, but that didn't mean he had to follow through. He could walk away. That would be for the best, and she had to make him understand.

And when she finally exhausted her spiel as they reached his door, he turned and smiled at her, and from the look in his face, she knew her entire speech had fallen on deaf ears. Had he heard a word she'd said? Or was he completely incapable of listening?

"Okay," he said. "I can see you're in no mood to be reasonable. But I have an idea." He looked much too happy about it, somehow. "You've told me time and again that you won't let me have my boy. I'm ready to concede that isn't going to happen. I don't have to be hit over the head with a two-by-four too often before I get the point." His voice hardened. "But I do have a fallback position. I hope you're ready to compromise."

She stared at him warily. "What do you mean?"

He opened the door and ushered her in. "I'm talking about a joint custody arrangement," he said simply. "We live together and both take care of the boy."

Her shoulders sagged. "You mean...?"

"Purely platonic," he said quickly. "An arrangement that satisfies us both."

She closed her eyes and felt suddenly very tired. "This is ridiculous," she said when she'd opened them again. " Can't you see that this is some fairy tale world you're concocting? People don't live like that. It's crazy."

There was no give in his expression at all. "People can live any way they damn well choose."

She frowned, shaking her head. "What makes you think I would agree to live with you without a marriage?"

He raised one dark eyebrow quizzically. "So you want to get married?"

"No! I do not want to get married." She turned, feeling a strange mixture of sadness and fury. She wanted to go home. She definitely did not want to be having this conversation. Turning back, she glared at him.

"You're going to have to face facts. This is my baby. He's growing in my body. I think it's going to be hard to find anyone who doesn't agree that I have the strongest claim."

He held her gaze. "Your claim may be stronger. But it's not complete. I've got a claim, too. And I expect to enforce it. We're both intelligent, caring adults," he said calmly. "We should be able to work something out that can satisfy both of us."

She looked away. "You make this sound like a business deal."

"Business deals are controlled by agreements made on paper and signed by both parties. That way, emotions don't get in the way."

He really was determined, and she was losing hope. "You're crazy," she said, stalking toward the entryway and reaching for her jacket. "I'm going home." She threw him a scathing glance over her shoulder as she pulled the door open. "You find another way to fulfill your daddying need," she told him. "You're a smart guy. I know you'll think of something." With her head in the air, she left.

But she knew her bravado was phony. The implications of this new wrinkle, his suggestion that they might live together and share raising Mikey, were just beginning to surface for her. He'd touched her tonight, touched her heart and soul in ways she wouldn't be able to erase. She was not going to be able to walk away from this and never think of him again. They were tied together now by more than this baby. Jack was in her life, one way or another. She was going to have to learn to deal with that, and very soon.

Chapter Seven

Jack sat drumming his fingers against the steering wheel of his flashy blue sports car, staring into space, thinking hard. The driver behind him gave a short honk and he looked up, startled. The light was green. He gave an apologetic wave and started through the intersection. His automatic reflexes were back into driving, but his mind was still on his problems.

He'd hardly slept. His mind had been churning all night long, going over one unworkable option after another. And every time, he kept coming back to the only thing that might work. Actually, it was Gayle who'd given him the idea. It sounded crazy, even to him. But she might possibly go for it. He was going to give it a go.

God knows, I've tried everything else, he thought.

Last night he'd thought living together and sharing custody might do it—of course, with the thought that she would tire of the arrangement eventually and give him full custody. He'd actually gotten a little excited about it. But once he'd brought it up, he'd known it wasn't going to fly. He had seen it in her eyes. And when he'd thought it through, he'd known it really wouldn't address all of his concerns, either.

Slowly, deep inside, he was coming to a realization. Much as it pained him and went against everything he'd vowed to himself, it looked like he was going to have to marry her.

She wasn't ready to face that any more than he was. And he didn't think that she was even beginning to reluctantly accept it the way he was. So that brought up another novel feature into their increasingly bizarre relationship. He was going to have to woo her.

He had to admit it wouldn't be all that tough. It wasn't as though she didn't attract him. In fact, it was almost embarrassing how much such an obviously pregnant woman could conjure up a physical reaction from him just when he least expected it. She'd knocked him back on his heels a couple of times. Sometimes it almost felt like being a teenager again. He couldn't figure out how he'd lost control of his hormones this way.

Control. That was the key. They had to make careful plans for this to work. He was lucky that Gayle was the quality person she'd turned out to be. Though it made his life more difficult, he grudgingly had to give her points for determination and commitment to her child. He would see if that commitment, which had been thwarting him all along, could be turned in his favor now that he had taken this new approach to solving their dilemma. In the meantime, he was going to have to practice up on his courtship style. Those old skills were definitely rusty from disuse.

"Let's see," he muttered to himself, pulling into the parking lot of a coquettish boutique. "Candy, cards, flowers. What else do women like?"

He turned off the engine and stared at the display window of the storefront before him. Lacy drapes were pulled open to reveal stuffed kittens and teddy bears cavorting with Cupid figurines. Scantily dressed fairy figures hung from above, swooping over the scene. Little inflated red and pink hearts floated everywhere. He shuddered. Thank God he was having a boy baby. Dirt and cars and sports equipment would be the order of the day once Mikey was born. But for now, he was going to have to delve into the feminine side of life for a while.

He opened the car door and stood up, feeling like a kid walking into the dentist's office. Bracing himself, he walked toward Cathy's Cute Collectibles. Unpleasant tasks were best done quickly.

Arriving back at work after a fun lunch in town with her friends at TriTerraCorp, Gayle knew something was up when she found a card propped against her computer monitor. Her name was written in a firm, crisp style she recognized as Jack's. Her breath came a little faster as she reached for it, and her heart beat high in her throat. She pulled the envelope open and looked at the card. Watercolor tulips fronted a handwritten message. "Thanks for joining me last night," it said. "You made me think. That never hurts." The card was signed, "Yours, Jack."

She stared at the handwriting, trying to analyze his true emotions from the way he'd formed his letters, until, realizing what she was doing, she threw the card down in disgust. No matter what he said, no matter how he acted, no matter how delicious his kisses were, he hadn't swerved from his main objective. He wanted her baby. And he wasn't going to get him.

Still, she smiled at Jack when they passed in the hallway, and she thought about him just about every minute of the day.

Later, when she went out to the parking lot to drive home, she found a pink rose tucked beneath her windshield wiper. She couldn't help but smile again. She was a woman, wasn't she? And she liked getting a surprise flower. How could she help it?

And when she arrived at her house, there was a huge box of candy tied with a beautiful organdy ribbon waiting on her doorstep.

"Jack Marin," she muttered to herself as she picked up the package and admired it. She couldn't keep down the glow that rose in her chest.

She made herself a small but nutritious meal and ate it slowly, watching a nature show on television. She didn't want to leave herself time to think. She'd done enough thinking. Now she was just going to go about having her baby and worry about the rest later.

She'd just washed up her dishes when the telephone rang. It was Jack.

"Hi. May I come over and see you?"

She swallowed down the excitement that threatened and managed to sound uninterested. "Um... why?"

"I'd like to talk to you."

She closed her eyes, fighting back the feelings his voice and words conjured up inside her. What was going on here? How had she let things get this complicated? Here she was, going through her days as though this were normal. It wasn't. She had to get out of this web Jack had her wrapped in.

She thought quickly. Time was of the essence. She ought to quit. She ought to leave town, just as she'd contemplated earlier. She had the Internet site set up to the point where another designer could easily take it over. If she didn't make a clean break now, she would never be able to. She was going to have to tell him. She had to go.

But at the same time, she knew thinking this way was useless. She was already too far into this. She couldn't run away now. But she could fight a little harder to maintain her own control over the situation.

She frowned, trying to make herself tougher. "We just spent an entire day only a few feet away from each other at the office. Why didn't you talk to me then?"

"You know we can't really communicate at work."

His voice was low and seemed to vibrate in a sexy way that made her crazy.

"Can't this wait till tomorrow?" she said, trying not to sound as breathless as she felt.

"No. I'll be over in about half an hour."

"Wait." Wasn't there some way she could stop him? No. she couldn't think of anything. "Do you know where I live?" she said, hating herself for being so pathetically weak where this man was concerned.

"Sure." He hesitated, then went on, his voice soft and husky. "I've been up and down your street a hundred times in the last few weeks."

Her eyes widened with shock. "What for?"

"Looking at your house. Thinking about you. See you soon."

She put down the receiver and took a deep breath. He was lying. He had to be lying. Her cheeks were blazing. She picked up her glass of iced tea and pressed it against her face. What was going on? This was insane. She had to put a stop to this right away.

She glanced at her reflection in the hallway mirror and stopped dead at what she saw. Her face was glowing. She looked downright beautiful.

"You love this, you faker," she said to her reflection accusingly.

And her reflection could only smile in agreement.

He sat in his car and stared broodingly at her house. He was rushing things, but that couldn't be helped. It would have been nice if they could have taken it slowly, but it wasn't like they had a lot of time to mull this over. Nature was taking its course and there was nothing either one of them could do about that.

He was going to have to pop the question tonight. Moving restlessly in his seat, he admitted his unease to himself. She was going to be surprised. She might even be outraged. She'd probably tell him to take a hike. If she was still deluding herself into thinking he might give up, she would probably be very upset.

And she had a right to be, in a way. He was rolling a month's worth of wooing into one day. Was it enough?

No, of course it wasn't. But what could he do? They had to get on with this thing, get it settled. From his perspective, he'd given her plenty of warning and plenty of time to get used to the situation. She ought to be ready to face reality by now.

But he knew damn well she wasn't. Hell, neither was he. He was only pretending to be. Because he had to. He had to make her see that marriage was the only way...for both of them.

She opened the door only a crack and stared out at him. He looked like a suitor with that bouquet of flowers in his hand. He was casually dressed in a white polo shirt that hugged his muscular chest, and faded jeans that were snug enough to provide proof he was a very fit man. Why was it that he looked better every time she saw him? She bit her lip. This was ridiculous. She was tempting fate in a reckless way she was going to regret. Wasn't there some way she could just get him out of her life?

"Are you going to let me in?" he asked.

"I don't know," she told him, her head to the side as she regarded him skeptically. And at the same time she wondered what he would do if she said No, if she stuck to it and closed the door and called the airport for a ticket out of town.

"We have a lot to talk about," he told her. "We could do it right here, if you want. But it might be more comfortable inside."

Funny how she could think of all sorts of reasons

to counter his moves when he wasn't around, but as soon as she was face-to-face with him, those ploys seemed to evaporate and she was left with nothing but the desire to see him and have him near. Still, she had to keep up a good front. "What can we possibly have left to talk about?" she said, though she knew as well as he did.

"There are whole mountains of things we still need to discuss," he told her evenly. "We haven't even begun."

She sighed. "All right. You can come in if you make me one promise," she told him, smiling ruefully.

"What's that?"

She looked him full in the face and said sternly, "No kissing."

His slow grin started and his eyes filled with amusement. "What have you got against kissing?"

"Kissing in general is pretty harmless," she told him, the slightest edge of teasing in her tone. "It's the kissing style that makes the difference. *Your* kissing should be categorized as brainwashing. There should be laws against it."

He laughed softly. "Okay. I promise. I'll only kiss you if you ask me to."

She opened the door to let him in. "I won't do that," she assured him, not really as confident as she sounded.

He brushed past her, gazing at her sideways. "We'll see."

She had a warm glow growing inside her and that wasn't good. She was going to have to be very careful. She took the flowers from him and gestured toward her living room, letting him find his own way. She went into the kitchen to put the flowers in water and brought back glasses for them both. They chatted for a few minutes, and then he asked questions about her marriage which she answered haltingly, but honestly.

"Your turn," she said after she'd had enough.

He looked startled.

"It's only fair," she added, giving him a look from under her eyelashes. "After all, you haven't told me much about your marriage."

"Haven't I?" he muttered, setting his glass of tea down and staring at it. "Lucky you."

"Come on," she coaxed. "I told you about my husband. Tell me about your wife."

He sat back and began to speak, but instead of talking about Kiki, he began to tell her about his childhood—growing up on the ranch out in the Santa Ynez Valley, chasing rabbits, learning how to care for horses, feeding the chickens, playing soldiers with his brother, Tony, in the irrigation ditches.

"I didn't know you had a brother," she said, her interest piqued.

"He died," he answered shortly, staring intently down into the ice cubes that were all that was left of his iced tea.

"Oh. I'm so sorry."

Glancing up, he saw compassion in her eyes, and it looked so real, so candid, that he smiled at her. "It happened long ago. He was eighteen. He was killed in a car accident."

"How old were you at the time?"

"Sixteen." He winced. "Tony was my hero. I miss him every day."

She nodded. "I know what you mean. It's hard to lose someone you love."

Jack glanced at her, wondering for just a moment if she was talking about her husband, if all her protestations about the lack of real love in her marriage had been a way of denying her pain.

But she seemed to read his mind. She sighed and added, "I felt that way when my father died. For a little while, I thought my world had ended. But you know, he's still so much a part of me, in a way, I feel like I've only grown closer to him over the years."

Jack felt a sense of relief, then shook it off, because it bothered him that he'd even felt it. Why should he care if she was really in love with her husband or not? He wanted to marry her, sure, but he wasn't in love with her or anything like that.

Romantic love was something he was never going to risk getting into again. There were enough threats to happiness out there in the world. You didn't need to ask for trouble.

"I have a sister," he told her. "Jana's married and lives with her husband and three children up in the Paso Robles area."

"That's not too far away."

"A couple of hours' drive. It's too far as far as my father and my aunt are concerned. They would like to see the kids much more often than they get to."

Gayle asked him more questions about his brother's death, but he changed the subject. He knew it frustrated her to have avenues of information cut off, but he just plain didn't want to talk about it. She was going to have to get used to that.

They talked for another half hour and then she showed him the room she'd prepared for her baby. It had none of the fancy elements his had, but it was sweet and comfortable. She could tell he liked the mobile she'd put up over the crib. Purple fish chased baby-blue seahorses around and around to the tune of a jaunty sea chantey.

They stood leaning against the side of the crib, and the feeling was very companionable as they talked about what Mikey would be like. Jack wound up the mobile again, and together they listened to the tune and watched the sea creatures bounce. Then he turned, smiled at her and touched her cheek.

She sighed and her eyes half closed. It was so tempting to give in to the impulse to enjoy his touch. But she knew where that would lead and she couldn't let it. Reluctantly, she pushed his hand away and took the opportunity to get back to the subject he'd avoided earlier on.

"Tell me what happened with your ex-wife," she said, turning to look into his face.

"What happened?" He shrugged. "The usual things," he said casually. "We were incompatible. We realized we had different goals in life. We went our separate ways."

Gayle cocked her head to the side and regarded him dispassionately. "Were you crazy in love with her at first?" she asked bluntly.

He stared at her, and then he had to laugh. "I

suppose I was," he said, shaking his head as though he just couldn't believe she'd said that. "What of it? That sort of thing doesn't last."

"Doesn't it?" She searched his eyes as though she really thought he knew the answer. "Are you sure?"

He took her hand in his. "Gayle, they have told you about the tooth fairy, haven't they? And the Easter bunny?"

"They say some people can sustain love over the long haul," she said earnestly, hoping her voice didn't betray her longing. "I've heard there are marriages like that."

He dropped her hand and turned away. "On Mars, maybe," he muttered, looking restless.

He was evading the issues again. If she let him get away with it, she was never going to find out the things she needed to know. There was too much mystery haunting his past, and the more she tried to clear it up, the more he seemed to avoid doing so. Her mouth was dry but she had to ask.

"Jack...what happened to the baby?"

He swung around, staring at her. "What baby?"

Her heart was beating hard in her throat. She knew he didn't want to go into this, but she had to push it. She had to know if her nagging suspicions were correct. "Jack, some of the baby things you have in that beautiful room you fixed up were bought years ago. I can tell."

"So what? That doesn't mean anything." But he looked restless and he wasn't meeting her gaze. He seemed to be on the verge of escaping once again.

She grabbed his arm. "Are you telling me there is no baby? You and Kiki didn't have a child?"

Looking down into her eyes he said emphatically, "I'm telling you exactly that."

"But she *was* pregnant, wasn't she?" Gayle wouldn't let go of his arm. She'd gone this far and she couldn't back down now. His eyes flashed with something that might have been pain and certainly was annoyance, and she recoiled.

"Oh," she said as the realization hit her. "Oh, she lost the baby. Is that it? Oh, Jack, I'm so sorry."

He seemed to wince and he looked away again. "It was years ago," he said gruffly. "It's long over. There's no use getting into it."

And that was that. He started another topic, talking quickly, leaving the issue of the baby behind with a sense of stern finality that left her sure there had to be more there. And yet he'd made it very clear he wasn't going to talk about it.

She followed him out of the baby's room and into the kitchen, where he began to raid her refrigerator.

"Got anything to snack on?" he asked. "I didn't have any dinner. I'm starved."

Reaching around him, she took hold of a carton of eggs. "How about an omelette?" she offered.

"Great."

They moved to the island in the center of the kitchen, and she began cracking eggs into a shallow bowl. He stood very close, gathering her silky hair into his hand.

At first she thought he was merely helping, trying to pull the unruly strands out of her way, but his hand lingered, and he was touching her hair and her neck in a manner too intimate for this to be a casual gesture of aid.

She turned her head and gave him a piercing look. "Jack, tell me something. Why are you here?"

His expression was open. "How can you ask? I want to be with you, of course."

She looked back down at the eggs she was cracking, one by one. "But why? We're not dating."

"Oh, of course not," he said, humor crackling in his voice. "We're not dating," he agreed, his hand sliding beneath her hair to cover the vulnerable area of her neck. "We're way beyond dating," he said softly, moving closer still. "We're having a kid together. You don't think that creates the sort of bond that needs nurturing?"

Her hands went limp. She hardly knew what she was doing any longer. His breath tickled her ear. His hand was creating heat all up and down her back. The sense of him so close, so warm, so large and masculine, was overwhelming.

She wanted to let herself sink into the sensual fog he was creating around her. It was so tempting to let this just happen. It was so delicious to have someone treat her like this. Especially someone like Jack—someone she was beginning to be very much afraid she could possibly fall in love with.

Had she really thought that? She shuddered, recoiling. There was no point in getting nutsy here. She had to keep her head.

Twisting away from him, she put up a hand as though to stop him. "I said no kissing," she reminded him warningly.

There was a sure and sexy gleam in his dark eyes. "Who's kissing?" he replied, all innocence, though he wasn't backing off. In fact, he was still moving closer, taking her shoulders in his hands and hovering over her in a way that set her heartbeat skittering.

But she shook her head and tried to be stern. "You're doing everything else but," she noted.

He looked pained. "You see, there you go. You should be a little more precise with your definitions." His fingers tightened on her shoulders and he drew her near again. "I believe the correct term for this is nuzzling," he murmured, as he proceeded to demonstrate into the cloud of hair at her neck.

"Jack!" She managed to twist away again, but she was half laughing. "I thought you were hungry," she said accusingly.

His grin widened. "Oh, I am. Can't you tell?"

"Jack!" She shook her head, her hair swirling around her shoulders. What was the use of pretending? "You know I'm susceptible to you."

His grin showed he did know it, and very well at that. "Do it," he urged her softly, reaching out to take her in his arms again.

"Do what?" She was almost panting and it showed.

He leaned closer, his lips almost touching hers. "Ask me to kiss you."

"No."

"Yes."

She sighed, surrendering, her eyes closing. "Kiss me," she whispered.

And he did, spilling warmth down her throat as though it were gold. She clung to him, all feeling, no thought. She'd never been kissed like this before. He made her feel like she was flying, lighter than air, soaring through a blue, blue sky. Vaguely, she realized he was speaking to her, and she blinked, trying to understand what he was saying.

"My beautiful, beautiful Gayle, the mother of my child," he murmured very near her ear. "Will you marry me?"

Her heart sank. He'd tricked her again. Gathering all her strength, she pushed him away. "Oh no, you don't," she cried, backing away from his touch.

"Gayle—"

"Out!" She pointed toward the door. "You're going."

"Gayle, wait a minute—"

She shook her head adamantly, her hair lashing back and forth like a whip. "No more, Jack. You've confused me for the last time." She pointed toward the door again. "Go."

He shook his head, half laughing, half apologizing as she drove him toward the door. "Gayle, wait." He hooked a corner of the table with his hand, holding on. "Let me explain. Just give me a minute."

She hesitated reluctantly, waiting to hear what he had to say, her eyes narrowed with a deep suspicion she didn't try to hide.

He smiled at her, his eyes warm and still bubbling with amusement. "I know this is something of a shock. You didn't expect me to decide on marriage after all I've said against it."

"You can decide on anything you want," she told him icily. "That doesn't mean I have to go along with it."

"I know that. And you know I've been just as opposed to marriage as you have." He shrugged helplessly. "But we've both said we would have to compromise. Haven't we?"

She nodded. "But marriage isn't compromise," she stated flatly. "It's surrender."

"But if we're surrendering to each other, that's compromise."

She shook her head. "I don't think so. I can't do that."

"You can't get married?"

"That's right."

He frowned, studying her eyes. "Why not?" he asked softly.

She wet her lips with the tip of her tongue. "Because…well, we're not in love."

He gave her a quizzical look, as though he really didn't buy that as an excuse. "That may be. But we do have a love interest in common."

"I don't think that is quite good enough."

"Gayle, listen—"

"No, you listen. I've been in a loveless marriage. I know what it's like. My husband loved me, and though I admired and respected him…and had a certain affection for him…I didn't love him. As time went by, I began to feel more and more guilty about it. Everyone said, 'Oh, you'll learn to love him as time goes by,' but it really didn't happen. That special closeness that you want to have with your life partner just wasn't there. The love wasn't there. And that began to eat away at our relationship."

Jack nodded. "I'm sure that can happen. But Gayle, that was just one pairing. You and he just didn't have the right chemistry." Reaching out, he took hold of her upper arm. "What do you think, Gayle? Do you think we have chemistry?"

There was no point in walking on eggshells with this man. "I know we do," she said bluntly. "But what we have between us isn't the sort of connection that lasts and you know it. Real love has chemistry but it's a lot more than that." As she said the words, she searched his eyes, looking for something and not really sure just what that was. She saw clouds and a flash of some emotion she couldn't identify. But she couldn't tell what he was really thinking.

He frowned and his fingers tightened on her arm. "How the hell did we get on this subject?" he growled. "We're not talking about love. We're talking about a man and a woman getting married because they both have a baby they love and want to nurture. That's all."

She shrugged, pulling away from his hand. "That's all," she agreed. "But that's too much."

He stood for a long moment, staring at her. Finally he seemed to make up his mind about something. "Tomorrow is Saturday," he said. "Come out to the ranch with me."

"The ranch?"

"I want you to meet my father and my aunt and see what it's going to be like for Mikey to live there."

His words twisted the knife in her heart. "Jack—" she protested.

He put a finger to her lips, stopping her words. "Regardless of what happens, Mikey will be spending time there," he reminded her. "You might as well come on out and see what it's like."

She swallowed, realizing he was right. "Okay," she told him. "But it doesn't mean anything."

His slow grin was back. "Of course not," he said lightly, giving her a wink as he opened the door and began to leave. "Pick you up at eight."

"In the morning?" she said with a grimace.

"Get used to it. When Mikey's here, you'll be up earlier than that every day." He stood on the porch and cocked his head to the side as he looked her over. "However, if we get married, I can handle the early morning detail. See? There are perks involved you never thought of."

"You?" She had to laugh at the thought of Jack up in his pajamas with a baby on his shoulder, ready to burp.

He sobered. "Hey, I intend to do my share of the work. I'm not planning to coast."

She watched him walk down the walkway toward his car, then she closed the door and leaned against it. He was wearing her down.

Chapter Eight

"Relax," Jack said, looking over and grinning at Gayle as she sat in the passenger seat, stiff as a board and apprehensive. "I promise I won't spring a surprise wedding on you unless you ask me to."

"That's what you said about the kissing last night," she reminded him. "You have a way of bewitching me and getting your own way, and you know it."

He laughed. He couldn't believe how happy it made him just to be riding along the highway—going home—with Gayle sitting beside him. The sky was blue, golden poppies were scattered across the green hills, the Pacific Ocean lay behind them, shimmering in the sunlight, and the tall, dark California oaks that marked the border of the ranch that had been in his family for six generations lay ahead. He didn't know how Gayle was going to react to his family, or his childhood home. Maybe she would be put off by his father's rugged gruffness, his aunt Trudy's good-natured nosiness, and his sister Jana showing up with her nerdy husband and their three wild kids. Perhaps Gayle would recoil and need to go upstairs to lie down and rest until they were gone again. That was pretty much the way Kiki had handled visits to his family when they were married. And maybe Gayle would do the same. Maybe not. At this point, he didn't really care. He just wanted to be home.

He turned off the freeway and started along the Solvang Road. "Look there," he said, pointing out a long white fence. "Miniature horses."

He slowed so that she could get a good look, enjoying it as her gasp turned into oohs and aahs.

"They are so cute," she cried. "I've never seen miniatures before. They look so friendly."

"They are," he assured her. "They'll come right up and sort of grin at you. They're very playful, too."

"We should get one for Mikey," she said, enchanted. "If we have room."

He went on driving, staring ahead at the road, waiting for her to realize what she'd said. Finally he glanced over to meet her gaze. She was wide-eyed.

"I...I mean..." Her voice trailed off helplessly.

He nodded. "I know what you mean," he said quietly. "We're almost there. Another two or three minutes."

"Oh." Her hand went to her hair. "Jack, what have you told them? About me and being pregnant and all."

He gave her a sideways grin. "I tried to think of a way to hide the fact that you're...in the family way…but telling them you're just a big eater isn't going to cut it, you know."

She rolled her eyes. "You're quite the comedian, aren't you? I'm serious. I want to be prepared for what they might expect."

He returned his attention to his driving. "I basically told them the truth. I said you were a good friend whose husband had recently died, that you were about to have a baby and that I wanted to bring you out to meet the family."

"So they don't know about…"

"That Mikey is mine?" He liked the spark of fire that flared in her eyes whenever he said something like that. He knew it annoyed her, but it also got her more and more used to the idea. "No, I didn't tell them that. Not yet."

She sighed. "I don't know whether that's good or bad," she murmured, more to herself than to him, and he nodded. He didn't know, either.

He turned on Marin Drive, and in another moment, the oaks came into view. He drove up the long driveway slowly, so she could get the full impact of the old stone house at the crest of the hill, the tall trees, the spectacular gardens currently spilling over with petunias and roses and nasturtiums. He knew she would never love the ranch like he did, but he wanted her to give it a chance.

For Mikey's sake, he told himself silently. But as he glanced over at the woman beside him, he knew it was more than that. For some crazy reason, he wanted her to love this place, too.

I shouldn't be this nervous, Gayle thought as she moved toward the man and woman coming across the grass to meet her. *These people are strangers. They really aren't going to be relevant to my life. Are they?*

The middle-aged woman reached her first, walking briskly, her short, plump body encased in denim gardening overalls, with tools sticking out of pockets and a sprayer set in a holster at her side.

"Welcome, my dear," she said cheerfully, though there was a wary quality to her smile. "We are so happy to meet any friend of Jack's."

She shook hands with Gayle, then turned to Jack's father, who had come along more slowly. "Anthony, this is Gayle Smith. Jack has brought her to spend the day with us."

"Glad to meet you," the older man said, though he hardly looked it. He shook hands with her as well, and she murmured polite greetings as she took in the whole of him.

The father seemed like an older version of Jack, but with such a sad look to him. His dark eyes with their thick, black lashes were beautiful, as beautiful as his son's, but they cut into her heart. A realization stabbed through her as she chatted with him about the drive. She didn't want Jack to ever have eyes filled with such tragedy. A part of her wanted to do whatever she had to do to make sure that didn't happen.

But that was a part that had to be squelched. Jack's future life had nothing to do with her. Why did she keep forgetting that?

"Come on," Jack said. "I'll give you a tour of the place."

He took her hand and escorted her through the gardens that his aunt cared for so lovingly. Stone paths led from one section to another. Various shades of green set off flower beds of every color and texture, while stone fountains and small statues graced different areas.

They stopped to rest on a wrought-iron bench set under a vine-covered arbor that gave a lovely view of the valley. Jack told her stories of childhood escapades that made her laugh. She looked at his handsome face as he talked. She'd never seen him look so happy. It was obvious he loved this place.

"Who makes the birdhouses?" she asked, looking around the area. Quaint wooden birdhouses of every size and shape hung nestled in among the greenery, and from the sound of it, the local birds were quite happy with them.

"My brother and I started the trend," he told her, plucking one from a tree and handing it to her for closer observation. "We made birdhouses in Boy Scouts. My father helped us and he got 'birdhouse fever.' Now he makes them for everybody we know. Give him a chance and he'll force you to take one home with you."

The birdhouse she held was yellow, with twining vines painted around it. Little doors on tiny hinges opened and closed. She'd never seen anything so precious.

"I hope he does offer me one," she said. Looking around, she listened to the birds, felt the wind on her cheek and wanted to spread her arms and dance in the sunlight, like some character in a musical. "Jack, it's so wonderful here."

"You really like it?" he asked, looking almost surprised.

"Oh yes. I love it."

His smile would have lit up a moonless night. "And you haven't seen half of it yet," he said, rising from the bench. "Come on." He held out his hand. "I'll show you the horses."

He showed her the horses and the cattle and the vegetable garden and the little vineyard where the grape stalks were just budding out with new green leaves. By the time they had seen all that, she was exhausted and hungry, and her shoes were a muddy mess.

"I guess we'll have to go down to the river later," he told her, taking in her condition. "You'd better get up to the house and rest."

She protested, but not very strongly, when he reached down and took her in his arms to carry her back up the hill. "Jack, I'm so heavy!"

"I know," he said, grinning. "Hold on tight. We'll be there in no time."

She held on tight, thinking how this was the third time he'd carried her since she'd met him. Why was he always going into this Sir Galahad act? she wondered. But as she pressed close to his warm skin and breathed in his clean scent, she had to admit that she liked it—liked it a lot. And without meaning to, without thinking, she leaned her face close to his neck and let her lips drop a small, fluttering kiss there. He stopped short, looking down into her face, and then they were kissing for real, tongues tangling, mouths hungry for shared tenderness, aching for satisfaction.

"Oh, Jack, no," she whimpered, pulling back. "We can't...."

He held her close and so tightly she could barely breathe. "We can do anything we damn well want to do," he told her, sounding almost angry.

And then he started walking again, holding her to him as she clung with her arms around his neck, while she wished with all her heart that what he had said was true. What if they really could do anything they wanted to? There were so many barriers in the way for them right now. And yet they seemed to have a bond between them. Was it just this baby she was carrying? If they had only met when they were both young and without other ties. Would it have felt this way? Would they have ended up in each other's arms, as though drawn together by an irresistible force? Or would they have smiled and talked and walked on by, not noticing that something deep and basic could bind them together?

Both of them had red cheeks by the time he set her down outside the kitchen entrance.

"My, you two look warm. Come on in and have some lemonade while I finish putting lunch on," Aunt Trudy told them, bustling back into her kitchen.

Jack's father was just coming in from the barn himself. "How do you like our place?" he asked Gayle as he stomped the mud off his boots.

"It's great. Jack tells me it's been in your family for many generations."

Anthony gave his son a piercing look. "Yup. Six to be exact. Though it looks like I might be the end of the line."

Jack's mouth took on a hard edge. "Dad..." he said warningly.

Anthony shrugged. "I know. It can't be helped." He looked at the obvious signs of Gayle's pregnancy, looked at Jack, frowned and shook his head before he started inside. But just when Gayle was sure he'd decided he disapproved of her, he stopped and turned back.

"I'll show you the 'Old Men' after lunch," he told her gruffly. "If you're a history buff, you might be interested."

"I'd like that," she said brightly, and then, when he'd gone into the house, turned to Jack and whispered, "Who are the 'Old Men'?"

He grinned. "My grandfather, my great-grandfather, my great-great-grandfather..."

"Oh." Her face cleared. "You mean your ancestors. Is it all the Marin family, or—"

"Only one certain line of the Marin family. Only the first sons and their wives."

"Ah. Like some sort of royal family."

"Exactly." He shook his head, bemused. "My father is a great one for innovations in ranching methods. He always has the latest computer available. But when it comes to the family hierarchy, he follows the pattern set down by another century." He shrugged. "And the rest of us adjust."

It occurred to Gayle that Jack was a second son. What affect had his brother's death had on that fact? She was about to ask him when Trudy stuck her head out the door.

"Lunch is almost ready," she said. "Come on in and get out of that sun."

Jack took her hand and smiled at her. "You hungry?" he asked.

Gayle let him lead her into the house, and wondered what his family thought of the two of them. They surely must be curious, but they were very polite and didn't make that obvious at all. The two of them walked through the kitchen and into the living room, where she gazed about with interest.

The house was very old-fashioned, but had been renovated by combining small rooms and opening up space to create large living areas. Oak wood and beveled glass was lightened by hanging plants and lacy curtains so that the ambience was fresh and bright rather than dark and gloomy as it might have been. Gayle had a feeling that was the result Aunt Trudy's influence.

"You have a wonderful touch with decorating," she told the older woman as they sat down in the dining room to a meal of crab salad and rosemary rolls. "I love the way you've filled this room with sunlight and color."

Trudy beamed with pleasure at the compliment and went on to describe in detail all the changes she'd made since she'd come to live with her brother about ten years before.

Trudy turned out to be quite a talker, which was convenient, because she didn't leave herself much time to ask questions, and answering them was something Gayle would just as soon not have done, anyway. So she listened and nodded and made sympathetic noises at the right times, and saw Jack and his father give one another significant, though affectionate, looks. Finally, as the meal disappeared into very satisfied stomachs all around, Anthony made a coughing noise to get her attention, then motioned for her to follow him as he got up from the table.

Gayle looked at Trudy. She was still talking. Gayle looked at Jack. He made a face and motioned with his head that she should go ahead and follow his father. It seemed he was ready to hold down the fort while she was gone. So she murmured her excuses, which Trudy gave no sign of hearing, and slipped away after Anthony.

She found him waiting for her in a hallway.

"I'm going back out to do some work in the stables and won't be back for a few hours," he told her gruffly. "Jack said you wanted to see the 'Old Men,' though, so I'd better get it over with now."

She followed him into a darker, high-ceilinged room that seemed to be the library. She had a feeling this was his own place, probably a refuge, at times, from his sister's conversations. The bookcases were filled with books from floor to ceiling, and between them hung large, gilt-framed portraits, most from another age, seven in all. Below five of the portraits were matching paintings of what must have been their wives.

"These are the ancestors," he told her offhandedly, making a sweeping gesture.

"Your forebears?" she asked, turning to look at them all.

"Yup. This here is General Victorio Antonio Marin. He got this place as a Spanish land grant in 1820." He pointed out a portrait of a stiff-looking man with a dark face who wore a uniform weighed down by pounds and pounds of gold braid. "And below him is his lady, Maria Elena.'' The woman was sharp featured and lovely, with lively dark eyes and a Mona Lisa smile. "Then we have their son, Antonio Carlos Marin, his son, Antonio Andrew Marin, with his wife, Carolyn Harding Moss, their son, Anthony the first, then Anthony the second, then me.''

"So Antonios turned into Anthonys," Gayle murmured, looking at the portrait of a younger Anthony. She noticed there was no corresponding picture of a wife set beneath his portrait, though there was plenty of room for one. But her attention lingered on his likeness. He had looked very much like Jack, but without the laughter in his face that Jack had. "And you must be Anthony Marin III," she noted.

"Right."

"And…" She realized, with a sudden pang of deep sorrow, that Jack's brother must have been Anthony Marin IV. There was a portrait in his place, a picture of a young man who looked a bit like Jack. What a tragedy to have lost him. "Oh."

"We have room for another Anthony," Jack's father said, looking at the one blank spot between bookcases. "But I don't know if we're ever going to fill it now." His sigh was deep and heartfelt. "This ranch has been handed down to the oldest son through the years. Every one is named Antonio or Anthony. It's our tradition. We've never wavered."

Gayle looked at his sad eyes and thought of what she knew of Jack. How did this tradition affect him? As she began to see how things were, she began to be angry. "Why not put up a portrait of Jack?" she asked carefully, working hard to keep her tone light. "He's the next in line, isn't he?"

The gray-haired man stared at her with unconcealed shock. "No, you don't understand. He's not a first son. He's not an Anthony," he said evenly. "It wouldn't be right."

"Wouldn't it?" she said, smiling brightly. "I think it would be perfect."

Stubborn as a mule, he shook his head. "This room is for the Anthonys," he said. "We got almost two hundred years of Antonios and Anthonys. We could put a portrait of Jack up someplace else. Not here."

He turned to go, and Mikey gave a kick so hard it almost took her breath away. That was when she realized what was really going on, and the realization stunned her. Her baby was supposed to be the next Anthony. Jack had never said a word about what he would like to name this baby, but she knew it as though he'd told her loud and clear. Outrage mixed with amazement. He might at least have mentioned it. It certainly did shed a little light on his quest for a baby. But even allowing for that, why would Jack go along with such a rigid tradition, when it seemed to her that it left him so in the lurch?

Gayle lifted her head when she heard a car door slam, and then the voices of children. She looked at the clock. She'd been sleeping for over an hour. Stretching, she yawned and looked around the room. There was a fireplace, a wardrobe instead of a closet, a huge mirror over the dresser, and best of all, a canopy over the bed. Aunt Trudy had told her it was a guest room, but it was furnished like a room that was used and loved. Gayle had had a nice rest and now it was time to go down and meet the rest of Jack's family, but she lingered a moment longer, thinking about the odd position she was in.

She'd begun to be a fierce partisan on Jack's behalf, and there was no reason for it—other than plain old idiocy. Sure she liked him—quite a bit, in fact. And sure, he was the father of her baby. But his relationship to his family was none of her business. So why did it make her so crazy to think that he let his father's obsession with this first-son name thing hurt him the way she knew it had to? She couldn't understand it. It was very sad that Tony, Jack's older brother, had died so young. But the family still had Jack, and it seemed to her they were very lucky to have him. He was, after all, a great guy.

Jana was terrific and Gayle liked her right away. Tall and beautiful, she had dark eyes that were copies of Jack's, and a bouncy vitality that seemed to be all her own. She'd left her husband behind—he was an engineer for a manufacturing company and he'd had a last-minute snafu that had necessitated his presence at work for the afternoon—and she'd brought her three children—two girls, six and four, and the boy, aged three. The two younger children spent a lot of time staring at Gayle's rounded belly, and finally they all three took turns touching it, awestruck by the thought of a baby making those bumpy places come and go.

Carrie, the youngest, looked up at Gayle apprehensively and put her face against the baby, laughing with delight when she felt it move beneath her nose. They were darling, well-behaved children, but they were full of energy and it made Gayle tired just watching them play. It made her a little worried, as well. Was she really going to have the strength to handle this little bundle of joy she was bringing into the world?

She and Jana helped Trudy prepare a lasagna in the kitchen. Anthony came in from the stables to greet the children, and Gayle couldn't help but notice that he and Trudy both lit up around them. They both seemed so much happier, coming alive as they interacted with them, and the children, sensing how much they were loved, acted like these two old-timers were their very favorite people. Maybe it was true, that children really did keep people younger. Altogether, it was a big, happy family, the sort Gayle had always dreamed of having herself. She envied Jack and wondered if he realized how lucky he was.

But there was still that nagging "downside," and she was worried about the things Anthony had told her in the library. She hadn't had a chance to talk to Jack about it, and she wondered if she should. On a whim, she brought it up with Jana when they were alone in the kitchen, while Trudy was in another part of the house, hunting down a magazine with a recipe for a dessert she wanted to try.

"Your father showed me the portraits of your ancestors," she said. "They were really interesting. It must be a nice thing to have roots that go so solid and so deep."

Jana stopped stirring the seasoned sauce long enough to groan. "He can lay it on pretty thick.

Don't pay him any mind. He may seem a little demented to the uninitiated, but when you get to know him, you'll realize he's not really a head case, after all.'' She smiled with quick affection for her father and went to the sink to wash off some sauce that had splattered on her hand. ''He's an old softy and a love, really. He's just been battered a bit by life's catastrophes.''

Gayle smiled in sympathy. ''You mean, your brother's death?''

Jana looked at her, wide-eyed, wiping her wet hands on her apron. ''Do you know about Tony?''

''I don't know much. I do know that he died very young.''

''Yes.'' She sighed, shaking her head as she went back to stirring. ''Well, you know, every family has to have its tragedy, and this is ours.'' She glanced around to make sure they were still alone before she went on. ''Tony died when a car ran a stop sign and plowed into the one he was in.''

''What a horrible thing for all of you.''

''Yes. He was the oldest son. I suppose Dad explained all that to you. The crazy old-fashioned traditions in our family make that very important. So Tony's death sort of threw everything out of kilter.''

She'd stopped stirring now and was looking at Gayle seriously, as though she was contemplating whether this person needed to know more or not. Seeming to make a quick decision, she went on.

''You see, Jack was driving our car. He was just sixteen. Tony was eighteen, and he was training Jack in preparation for taking his driver's test.'' She shook her head, remembering. ''You know these country roads. People drive so fast on them and think they can ignore the laws. So a speeding drunk ran the stop sign and hit our car, and Tony was killed instantly. Jack didn't have a scratch." She looked deep into Gayle's eyes. "Do you understand what that did to Jack? He took all the guilt onto himself. Not only did he lose a brother that he loved more than anything, he also carried the guilt of being the one driving when it happened."

Gayle felt the room begin to rock and she leaned against the counter to steady herself. "But you said it wasn't his fault."

"It wasn't. But tell that to him." She shrugged. "To make matters worse, Tony was our mother's fair-haired child, the apple of her eye. When he died, her grasp of reality sort of slipped away. She couldn't take it anymore, and she took off."

"She left?"

"Yup. Left her two remaining kids and grieving husband behind and headed for the lights of the big city. Nice, huh?" She grimaced, looking out the window at where her children were playing. "I didn't understand it then, and I can't understand it today. I would die myself before I'd leave those precious kids of mine to face things alone." She turned and gave Gayle a quick smile. "But that's neither here nor there. I've probably told you more than you ever wanted to know, but I figured, since you're such a good friend of Jack's, you ought to have the truth. He can be a moody guy sometimes, and now you have some idea why."

Gayle reached out and put her hand on Jana's arm. "Thank you," she mouthed, as Trudy came back into the kitchen. What Jana had told her did explain a lot. And her feelings for Jack were growing by leaps and bounds. Why was it that everything new she learned only made her care about him more?

Before dinner, Jack led Gayle out along a road cut so that she could see the place where he'd first discovered fossils and his love for geology was born. Then he took her down to see the river, his special place all the years of his boyhood.

"We went swimming here in the summer," he told her, his eyes crinkling with the memories. "We built forts along the side, over there. We had wars here, attached ropes to tree branches and swung out over the water, went fishing, sailed boats. This was the greatest playground any kid ever had."

She looked up and down the waterway. Clear water ran over golden rocks, and pepper tree branches hung low over the stream, making a lovely picture of rural tranquility.

"All in all, you seem to have had a pretty happy childhood," she noted.

He looked surprised at the statement. "Happy? Sure. Most of the time." His eyes changed as he took her by the hands and pulled her closer. "Do you like it here?" he asked her softly, looking down into her face as though her answer really mattered to him.

"At the ranch?" She nodded happily. There was no point in trying to hide it. "I love it here. It's wonderful."

He laughed and pulled her closer still. "Gayle Smith, you've got to marry me," he told her, gazing deep into her eyes.

She stood with her head tilted back so that she could see into his face. "Jack Marin, I've already told you that is impossible."

"Nothing is impossible. All you have to do is set your mind to it."

She laughed softly. "In other words, do it your way."

"Why not call it 'our way'?"

"Because," she said, trying to be as gentle as possible, "it's my baby. That's why."

He frowned. "I think you're being selfish," he said.

"What do you mean?" she asked, startled.

He raised one eyebrow. "You want Mikey all for yourself. You want to gather in all the love and not have to share it with anyone else." He shook his head as though he were trying to understand her motivations. "Are you that hungry for love?"

"You've got it all wrong," she told him softly, wishing she had the words to explain so that he could see it from her point of view. "It's a matter of control, not love."

He didn't understand. Frowning, he shook his head. "Control? Control of what?"

She tried to think of a way of explaining it to him. Pulling away from him, she gazed down into the swirling water. "Jack, don't you see? I could so easily be pulled into your world. But I don't think that should happen. I need to keep control of what is happening to me—and to my child. When I was married to Hank, I was like a child myself, doing whatever he told me I should be doing. I can never give up my autonomy like that again."

"Of course not," Jack agreed, looking chagrinned that she would even think such a thing. "And I wouldn't want you to do anything of the sort." He tilted up her chin and dropped a quick kiss on her lips, surprising her. "But don't you see? This isn't a matter of control at all." His voice had a strain of sincerity she couldn't deny. "Gayle, I want to protect you. And Mikey. And the best way to do that is to marry you."

For all her brave words, she was weakening. Could he sense it? Probably. She looked up into his handsome face and admitted to herself that there were worse fates waiting out there than to be married to this man.

"Just…just exactly what kind of marriage are you talking about?" she asked him.

His eyes lit with a spark of triumph. He knew she'd allowed a chink in her armor. But he tried to remain casual, and he shrugged. "Sort of…well, maybe a marriage of convenience, I guess you could call it. At least to begin with."

She frowned, concerned and slightly embarrassed—though she would die before she would let him know that. "One of those polite, just-friends, no-sex arrangements?"

His face registered a shadow of distaste. "Well…"

"Because you know that's out of the question," she added quickly.

He looked confused. "What do you mean?"

"Sex. We can't have sex." She watched his eyes, feeling breathless, knowing that she was dying for him to grab her and tell her that was ridiculous—that he wanted her and wanted her now. That he couldn't get her out of his mind....

She took a deep breath, realizing she had better settle down.

She was eight months pregnant, for Pete's sake! Pregnant women didn't have men panting after them, did they? No, of course not. The trouble was, pregnant women were still human. And when she looked at Jack, she had a better idea of what real desire was than she'd ever had before. Funny. Sex with Hank had never been any big deal. But just the thought of intimacy with Jack made her shiver inside.

She tried to remember what it had been like with Hank. Had she ever felt with him the way she felt with Jack? It had been so different then. Hank had just been around, so familiar, so comforting—always there. And when she lost her father, she'd been so scared of losing him, too, that when he suggested they marry, it had seemed like a godsend at the time. She'd been so young then. It was only later that she realized how unfair it had been to marry a man she really didn't love—unfair to him, unfair to her. She'd had a lot of affection for Hank, but she'd never really loved him—never really been *in* love with him. She thought now, from the evidence, that he had probably been in love with her. But he hadn't been able to articulate it. Or demonstrate it much, either.

But she was waiting to hear what Jack was going to say. She could see that there was conflict going on inside him. She put a hand flat against his chest and felt the beating of his heart. It felt so right, as though it were beating in time with hers. He'd pulled her so close that his breath was teasing her hair. She was melting against him, feeling an urge to get as near as she could. She remembered the kissing and knew she was an addict. All she wanted was more. All she wanted was Jack.

"Okay," he said softly, his eyes dark as melted chocolate. "No sex. Until you ask for it."

She gasped, but his mouth was on hers and she didn't have time to complain. For a few minutes, words faded and only feelings ruled. The sense of warmth, spiced by a controlled urgency that underlay it all, sent her reeling once again. And by the time the kissing was over, and they were walking back to the house, she'd forgotten that she had any complaint to make. While he was taking detours off the path, throwing a stick for the dog to chase and calling to the kids at the house, she was busy wondering if she would be a crazy fool to marry this man.

And if she did marry him, could she love him?

"Oh, yes," she whispered, folding her arms around her and hugging herself, hugging her new knowledge of herself and of what she could so easily feel for this man. "Oh yes, most definitely."

The question was, could *he* ever love *her?*

They stayed longer than they'd planned, helping with the dishes, talking and laughing with Jana, playing Twister with the children. It was late when they finally gathered up the leftover lasagna for Jack, the three cute little birdhouses Jack's father had given Gayle and the pictures the girls had drawn for the baby. Jack packed everything in the car, waved and called goodbye as they headed down the driveway and turned toward Rio de Oro. Jack glanced over at her and smiled. She looked happy. In fact, she looked about as happy as he felt.

"Did you have a nice time?"

"I had a wonderful time," she told him candidly, stretching back in her seat. "I think you have the nicest family in the world."

"I like them pretty much," he admitted. "It's a pretty good family. There's only one thing missing."

"What's that?" she asked, though she was pretty sure she knew.

"You."

She winced. "Jack. Don't."

"Don't what?"

"Don't pressure me."

He gave a sound of exasperation and pulled the car over into a turnout overlooking the ocean. Switching off the engine, he swung around to gaze at her in the dark.

"There's only one way to get me to stop pressuring you," he told her calmly. "And you know what that is."

"Having your lips sutured shut?" she asked lightly, looking out at the moonlit waves.

He shook his head. "That won't do it. I can pressure without words."

She laughed softly. "I'll bet you can."

He gripped the steering wheel with both hands. "Tell me what's holding you back."

"I've already explained that to you." She looked at him and sighed. "I don't want to have another loveless marriage."

He frowned. "It doesn't have to be like that."

"Doesn't it?" She stiffened her spine and asked

the appropriate question. "Do you love me, Jack?" she said, challenging him.

He was silent for much too long for the answer to be anything but no. She wanted to point that out to him, but for some reason there was a lump in her throat. He didn't love her. But she already knew that. Why had she asked such a stupid question?

"You don't love me. The last time you married you were wild about your wife, and it didn't work out. Now you want to try again, even though—"

"Gayle..."

"Admit it. You were crazy about her, couldn't-live-without-her in love, weren't you?"

"Maybe. So what?"

"Well, you don't feel that way about me right now, do you?"

He grimaced, looking uncomfortable. "I'm not a kid anymore."

"I know, but..."

Turning, he reached out and touched her hair. Then he let his hand glide down to her shoulder, his dark gaze following.

"Gayle," he said, his voice strained. "I want to care for you and my baby. I want to make a home with you both. I want a place that's secure, loving and full of joy every day." He looked into her eyes. "My first marriage was a disaster, even worse than yours. Things happened between me and my wife that I still can't think about without it hurting. I always vowed I would never, ever risk going through that again." He took a deep breath and held her gaze with his own. "But now I'm going to risk it. I come to you with my heart in my hands. It's all I have to give. Please accept it.''

Tears welled in her eyes and she blinked hard, trying to get rid of them. She was dying to fall into his arms, but she couldn't let herself be overwhelmed by his appeal. She had to stay tough—if she could.

"Jack," she answered, her voice choked. "We both know you only want to marry me to have full rights to Mikey. If I weren't having your baby, you wouldn't look twice at me."

A flash of something similar to pain crossed his handsome face. "That's not true."

"Yes, it is. But you know what?" Reaching out, she cupped his cheek with her hand and gazed lovingly at him. "I'm going to marry you anyway. That might make me the biggest fool in the county. But I'm ready to take a chance if you are."

He stared as though he couldn't believe what she'd said. "Are you serious?"

She nodded. "Yes, Jack. I'm serious."

Grabbing her hand, he pressed his lips to her palm, closing his eyes. She closed her eyes, too, but though he was saying a silent prayer of gratitude, she was saying one of apprehension. She was making a very dangerous leap into the unknown and she was going to need all the help she could get.

Chapter Nine

Getting married was a pain in the neck. At least, that was the way it looked to Gayle. When she'd said she would marry Jack, she'd envisioned a quick visit to a justice of the peace and then maybe a quiet dinner out to celebrate. She had seen no reason why anyone even had to know about it. At least not right away.

"We can't do this behind my family's back," Jack had protested when she'd mentioned it the next morning. They were plotting strategy while walking on the bike path that meandered along the shoreline. The morning fog had receded, but a cool marine breeze was blowing, holding back the heat of the sun. "They would be hurt if we didn't let them get involved."

"Oh." Of course, he was right. She just wasn't used to having an extended family to consider.

"Then there are all my employees at the firm."

Gayle gaped at him, aghast. "Why do we have to tell *them*?"

"I think we'd better." He pulled her out of the way of a tall girl on Rollerblades who zipped past, braids flying. "I'll make the announcement first thing tomorrow morning."

Gayle frowned, apprehensive. She pulled her sweater closer and looked out across the sand at the breaking waves. "Can't I just silently slip away and disappear from the scene?" she asked, her yearning in her voice.

"No. I'll be disappearing, too." He seemed thoroughly amused by the prospect. "With us both disappearing at the same time, people are bound to notice. It will look very strange. There's bound to be talk."

His teasing went right over her head, because she was still stuck on his first statement. "Why will *you* be disappearing?"

"Hello." He pretended to knock on her door. "Remember me? We're getting married on Saturday."

"I know. Why does that set off a disappearing act?"

"Because I'm taking a leave from the business." He shoved his hands into the pockets of his jeans, looking very comfortable with his decision. "Betty is up to speed and can run things for me for a while. And I can come into town if there's anything shaking. That way we can both go out and stay at the ranch. That will be much more comfortable for you. Plus we'll have plenty of help when we want it, and at the same time, we can stay in our own section of the house most of the time." He glanced at her to see if she was receptive to this idea. "We could even stay for a few months after Mikey is born, and move back into town to my condo when you feel you're ready. We'll play it by ear."

"Oh." She had to admit it sounded lovely, like an extended vacation. She really had enjoyed the ranch. The thought of living there, far from the rat race and all that went with it, was enticing. It just gave her one more thing to look forward to.

But by Tuesday, she was beginning to feel she would need a real vacation after all the planning for the wedding was over. Now she was up to her eyebrows in catalogs for flowers, and making arrangements for ministers and hiring a chapel and deciding whether she wanted to wear a gown. It seemed a bit much. After all, this was supposed to be a marriage of convenience. Sort of. And still there were so many decisions. What to wear? What to carry? Something old, something new, something borrowed, something blue? Should a pregnant bride wear white? And a veil?

But Jana took that decision right out of her hands.

"I've got a wonderful seamstress. She made my wedding gown. She says it will be no problem to take my dress and open it up and sew in another panel to accommodate that little wiggler you're carrying out in front of you."

Gayle was shocked. She'd had nothing but welcome from Jack's family, and Jana had been especially nice, calling her right away to express her joy at the news. But loaning out her own wedding gown? That seemed almost too much.

"Jana, that's so nice of you, but I was planning on wearing an ivory suit I've had—"

"Don't be silly. This is going to be a very special day and you need a very special dress to help create the mood."

"But don't you want to save your dress for your daughters?"

"No. I want it for my brother's bride."

What could she say at that point, but "Thank you so much"?

Jana was a big help in the preparations. She and her children had decided to stay at the ranch all week so that she could help with the arrangements. She was the one who talked to the church scheduler after Gayle had been told that they were booked solid for the next six months. Jana managed to cajole an hour on the following Saturday for their service, promising that the decorating and ceremony would be quick and the cleanup afterward would be thorough.

"Along with a nice contribution to the church charity fund, no doubt," Jack said with a grin when Gayle told him about it at the office the next day. "I'll have to make sure she gets reimbursed."

But the biggest shock was on Tuesday when Gayle walked into the lunch room at work and found it filled with practically every woman she knew.

"Surprise! Surprise!" The shouts nearly bowled her over, and she stood in stunned amazement.

Balloons and streamers filled the air along with the shouts. There was a table piled high with food, and another piled even higher with presents. Chareen and Kyra came out of the crowd to hug her.

Gayle greeted them warmly. "I can't believe you

all did this," she kept repeating, looking about her with awe.

"We were planning to have a baby shower for you, anyway," Kyra told her. "So we just added a wedding element and created a double shower. Enjoy!"

"Right," Chareen interjected. "Baby, wedding...wedding, baby, what the heck. It's all the same."

They led her over to the couch that had been placed as the focal point, facing folding chairs set in a semicircle. Gayle smiled at all her friends, feeling very touched, but they were all talking at once and it was hard to know which conversation to follow.

"You really surprised us," Phyllis was saying, shaking her head.

"Yeah!" Cissy chimed in. "But I didn't think...well, I mean, it's only been a few months since...well, you know..."

Everyone glared at her and she retreated helplessly, apologizing.

But she was right. This was awfully soon after Hank's death to be marrying again. Still, Gayle couldn't let it bother her that some people might not like it. She had her baby to consider.

Jill stepped in to take her side. "I think it's wonderful and I guess you wanted to hurry so you could bring the baby into the world with a ready-made dad, didn't you?" she said, preparing to glare a challenge at anyone else who might want to criticize her decision.

Gayle flashed her a quick smile. "That's just about it," she admitted.

She nodded. "I think that's really a good thing to do."

The murmur that went around the room backed her up.

"You're really lucky that you found such a great guy," Billie said with a wistful smile.

"I am very lucky," Gayle said in agreement. "And I'm lucky to have such great friends as you all are, too."

They all spoke at once for a moment, then one voice piped up above the rest. "Gayle, where's the ceremony going to be?"

"Jack's family have a church they attend out in the Santa Ynez Valley. It has a little wedding chapel attached, Chapel of the Angels. Members of his family have been getting married there for over a hundred years."

"How nice," several voices murmured.

"I wish I could invite you all, but we're planning on just family." Gayle smiled apologetically. "It's a tiny little chapel, from what I hear."

"Are you going on a honeymoon?" Billie asked hopefully.

Gayle's smile froze for just a moment. After all, honeymoons were for people who were desperately in love. She couldn't claim that she and Jack were that. A honeymoon would be most inappropriate, considering.

But her friends didn't really need all the gory details, so she shook her head, patting the baby bulge she carried, and declared, "We don't dare. Chances are we'd start out as a couple and come back with an extra member." She laughed along with her friends. "This little critter is only a few weeks away from waking up and making his debut. I want to be home when that happens."

The party went on for another hour. They didn't have time to play more than one shower game, because the presents had to be opened and the club sandwiches eaten and the cake cut. Gayle felt warm and honored by her friends, and slightly bewildered by it all.

Then she looked up and saw Jack standing across the hallway, watching through the glass. Her gaze met his and locked, and she suddenly felt grounded again, connected to something secure and right. For just a moment, she was very sure she was doing the right thing.

But the moment didn't last. Suddenly she realized that she was marrying a man she hardly knew, a man whose first marriage she still didn't have enough details of. A man who didn't love her. Was she crazy?

She *was* crazy—about him. But he wasn't crazy about her. She knew he liked her. They had a nice bond of affection, but she'd had that with Hank. And that hadn't, in the end, been enough. Was this going to be like her first marriage, only reversed? Was she going to be the one who loved with all her heart and yet couldn't get what she wanted from him? Was he going to eventually yearn to break free of the bonds they were planning to bind about them? She wasn't sure she would be able to stand that.

But what could she do? She had her baby to think of. She knew that the only reason he was marrying her was because of Mikey. But he'd been honest. He'd never pretended otherwise.

If only she could be as cool and detached as he was. Somehow she had let her heart get involved, and that threatened to make it a marriage more of *in*convenience—at least for her.

The time seemed to fly by, and suddenly it was only hours before the wedding. Gayle lay in her bed and stared at the ceiling, listening to the clock tick the time down. Jack was picking her up early in the morning and they were driving out to the ranch. Jana had a hairdresser hired, and the dress was supposed to be ready, seamstress at hand for any needed alterations on the spot. At four in the afternoon, the wedding would take place. Afterward, they would go back to the ranch and have a celebration of some kind. Gayle wasn't sure of the details. This was going to be one of the most important days of her life. Just thinking of it made her heart thud loudly.

"Sleep!" she ordered herself. "You've got to sleep. You can't get married with circles under your eyes."

But sleep seemed further away all the time. Her mind was racing, wondering what on earth she was doing. There was so much she wasn't prepared for.

She tossed and turned, and finally, she gave up. She wasn't going to sleep. There was no use pretending. She had some questions, a few things she really needed to know if she was going to do this thing. And if she was going to do anything about finding out the answers to her questions, she would have to work fast.

Slipping out of bed, she reached for her clothes. She was going to go right to the horse's mouth on this one. It was much too late for visiting, but she was going to make a call, anyway. She only hoped that, once she got to his place, she could wake Jack up so that he would let her in.

Luckily, it seemed he wasn't a very heavy sleeper. She rang the doorbell three times before he made it to the door and opened it. That wasn't too bad. It certainly could have been worse. She was in no condition to climb up and hoist herself over his balcony railing.

"Are we crazy?" she demanded of him. "We can't get married tomorrow. We don't even know each other."

He ran a hand through his already tousled hair and blinked at her sleepily. "Gayle…do you know what time it is?"

"Absolutely." She stood with her hands on her hips and her chin tilted at a challenging angle, trying not to notice that he looked extremely sexy in his hip-hugging pajamas and bare, beautifully muscular chest.

He yawned. "Come on in," he said with sad resignation, opening the door just wide enough to let her in. "You can sleep on the couch."

"I didn't come here to sleep." She came inside, closing the door behind her, then realized he was heading off toward the back of the condo. "Wait. Where are you going?" she cried after him.

"To bed," he said, not looking back at her. "It's two in the morning." And he disappeared into the hall.

"Jack!"

Charging down the hallway, she followed him into his bedroom. The only light came from the hall, but she could make him out. He hadn't hesitated, but was climbing right back into bed, pulling the covers up to his chin and closing his eyes.

"Good night," he mumbled groggily, snuggling in. "Sleep tight. Don't let the bed bugs bite."

She stood over him with her hands on her hips. "Jack, we have to talk."

"Later."

"No, now!" She dropped down on the edge of his bed and shook his shoulder. "Wake up. This is important."

He groaned, finally opening his eyes, even if only as slits. "Do you do this a lot?" he asked blearily. "Because if you do, it might be cause for an annulment. I hate waking up in the middle of the night."

"We won't need an annulment if we never get married."

He frowned, considering her last statement. "Hey, you're right," he agreed. "Okay. Let's not get married." Closing his eyes, he looked perfectly ready to fall asleep again instantly.

"Jack, we have to talk." Sighing, she flopped down beside him. Her stomach was too big to let her lie on it, but she edged onto her side instead, holding up her head with one hand while she gazed at him. "I've been thinking, and it is insane for us to try to get married. We don't know each other well enough to form a business partnership, much less a lifelong relationship that's going to determine how we live our lives for the next twenty years—and how we manage our baby's life."

He made a sound. She stared at him, trying to ascertain whether or not he was still awake. That had either been a grunt of derision or a snore. She wasn't sure which.

"Jack, wake up," she demanded, shaking his shoulder again. "There are so many things we don't know about each other. For instance, did you know that I hate cottage cheese? That my favorite movie is the *Philadelphia Story* with Katherine Hepburn? That I love to cha-cha? That when I was growing up, my nickname was Pookie?"

He finally showed signs of life. One eye opened, just a little. "Pookie?" he echoed.

"See?" She threw up her hands. "That proves my point. You don't know the first thing about me. Most people who get married have months and months to feel each other out and find out if they are compatible. We haven't had that."

He propped his head up and gazed at her with clouded eyes. His bare shoulders were gleaming in the muted light from the hallway. She couldn't help but let her gaze linger on them for a moment. He was so deliciously sleek and golden.

"What do you suggest?" he asked her, his tone a bit sarcastic. "Shall we tell Mikey to hang in there for a few months until we're ready for him to come out?"

She bristled. "Of course not. I know it's an unreasonable complaint in a lot of ways. But…but Jack, there is one thing I am very worried about. I really feel I can't marry you until…" She took a deep breath and charged ahead. "Until I know more about what happened between you and Kiki. What ruined your marriage.''

Throwing his head back, he groaned. "We've already exhausted that topic."

"Jack, I can tell there's more than what you've told me. And I know it's your private life. But if I'm going to be a part of that life, I think I have to know."

He was silent so long, she was afraid he'd gone back to sleep. Finally, he spoke. "You're right, Gayle. You have a right to know everything. And I'll tell you as much as I can. But we'll never talk about it again. Okay?'

"Of course."

"Okay." He took a deep breath, lay back, threw his arm over his eyes and began to speak. "Kiki was beautiful and exciting and a lot of fun. I wanted babies right away. She kept putting off having them. She got very involved in charity work. Joined all the right clubs. And after a while, she was gone all the time, working on fund-raising events and putting on shows for charity. I hardly noticed, because I was working so hard starting up my business. She had an affair with a guy in one of her organizations."

Gayle closed her eyes and bit her lip.

"I heard about it from a friend," Jack continued, "and I confronted her. She cried and claimed it was because I was ignoring her. I forgave her, asked her to forgive me. She quit all the clubs and came to work for me at the office. Everything seemed to be okay. And when she got pregnant, I thought we were over the hard part, that having a baby would really settle her down."

Gayle opened her eyes and turned her head to look at his profile, or what she could see of it. The fight to remain objective was over. She adored this man. She wanted to fend off any pain that might threaten him in any way. And yet she had to hear what he had to tell her, so she remained quiet, waiting.

"I was deliriously happy about the baby," he told her, speaking more softly now. "I sort of jumped the gun, buying out the town, fixing up the baby room that you saw. I was so happy doing that, I didn't notice that she wasn't joining in on the fun. And then…"

His voice was strained and he cleared his throat before going on.

"And then one day I came home from work and found her coming out the door with suitcases. I was stunned. I'd had no idea…." He took a deep breath. "She told me she and Jerry—my partner—were in love. They were going away together. And she'd gotten rid of the baby."

Gayle gasped. "Oh, Jack."

"I was… I don't know that there is a word for what I was. She left with Jerry. I heard they lasted about six months before he was cheating on her. Now I think she's married to a doctor in upstate New York. But we were completely over as far as I was concerned the moment she told me what she did to our baby."

Gayle wanted to reach out to him, to hold him in her arms, but she could sense that he would reject her comfort right now, so she resisted.

He removed his arm and turned to look at her. "Okay. Now you know. Can we go to sleep?"

She hesitated, wanting to talk more but knowing he didn't want to. Finally she nodded. "I'll go out and sleep on the couch."

"No." His hand shot out and caught her arm. "You stay right here," he told her huskily. "You can even get under the covers."

"But, Jack—"

"Don't worry." He touched her cheek with his cupped hand. "I'm not going to do anything. But I want you near me. Okay?"

"Okay," she whispered, and did as he'd asked.

She lay in his arms, feeling his even breathing against her neck, feeling a growing sense of belonging. She'd found out what she'd felt she had to know. She'd been afraid it might be something that would send her running for the exit in this relationship. But instead, she now knew more about what made this man tick. She wasn't panicked any longer. She was going to marry him, and she was glad.

Finally, she slept.

The wedding march was peeling through the chapel. Gayle took a deep breath and got ready to make her way down the aisle. The chapel was bigger than she'd been led to believe and the pews were filled with all her friends. Somehow it didn't surprise her that Jack had invited them just to please her. She took one last look at herself in the full-length mirror. A pearl-studded tiara held the veil that fell in lovely folds around her face. The gown had turned out to be perfect, antique white lace and satin and lots of seed pearls. Her bouquet was huge, a thousand tiny white flowers as a setting for the biggest violets she'd ever seen. Pregnant or not, she looked pretty darn beautiful, even if she did say so herself.

Turning, she stepped briskly toward the aisle, where Jana waited. Jana's girls were going ahead, strewing rose petals from their Easter baskets, pretty as pictures in their yellow dresses and white lace tights. And down at the end of her journey was Jack, looking incredibly handsome in his tuxedo with the white silk cummerbund, his dark hair combed more carefully than usual, his dark eyes shining. He thought she was beautiful, too. She could see it in his eyes as she joined him at the altar, and that made her glow with a special joy. She was getting married. And this time it was to a man that she loved.

"Do you take this man...?"

Oh, she did! She really, really did. The ceremony was ethereal to her. She thought she could hear angels singing. The afternoon sunlight slanted in through the stained glass windows, and it seemed to her that it was enchanted, dusting the whole congregation with a blessing from above.

Jack slipped the ring on her finger and she stared down at it in wonder. How could a simple gold band look so incredibly beautiful?

"I now pronounce you man and wife."

She turned toward Jack and searched his eyes, wanting so badly to see love. He smiled, and she saw happiness, and tenderness, and even affection. *Never mind,* she told herself quickly. *Never mind.* Maybe it was enough.

"You may kiss the bride."

He lifted her veil and leaned toward her. She held her breath. Then his lips were on hers and the world fell away and it was only the two of them, holding fast to one another as the room spun around them, the golden sunlight spilling over them, the music swelling in the background.

Hold tightly to this, she told herself silently as she let herself be swept away by the magic. *This is a moment you will want to cherish in your heart forever.*

Too soon the moment was over. As they walked back up the aisle, waving and smiling to their friends, she held on to his hand as though she would never let it go again.

Chapter Ten

The baby was coming. Gayle lay very still and felt her stomach turn hard as stone, and she knew. Mikey was coming tonight.

"Hang in there, sweetie," she whispered to her baby. "Buckle up. It's going to be a bumpy ride."

She heard the old grandfather clock in the lower hallway strike midnight. Should she go into the next room and wake Jack? Not yet. Let him get another half hour of sleep. After all, she knew how much he hated to be woken in the middle of the night. She smiled to herself. Something told her that this time he wasn't going to complain.

She switched on the bedside lamp and reached for the pad of paper and pencil she had ready, jotting down the time. Once the contractions seemed to be spaced regularly, she would call her doctor. In the meantime, she would just wait. Settling back into her covers, she smiled happily. Mikey was coming. By this time the next night, she would have her baby in her arms.

It had been a wonderful few weeks out here on the ranch. She and Jack had their own suite of rooms, on the opposite side of the house from where Trudy and Anthony slept, so they had all the privacy they could want. In the mornings, Jack went down and fixed breakfast for them both, bringing it up onto the balcony, where they ate a leisurely meal while watching the horses in the compound and listening to the birds sing. After a shower and a quick cleaning of their area, Gayle would go down to see if she could help Trudy with anything. Lunch would usually find the four of them eating together, and in the afternoon Jack would take her to shop in Solvang or to see the miniature horses or to ride out to the lake. In the evenings they sometimes ate out, or had visitors. On a few nights, she and Jack attended the childbirth classes Vicky had set up for her.

Gayle snapped back to the present when another contraction started. It was a hard one. She went into her breathing routine, carefully breathing in and out and rubbing her belly lightly with her fingertips. As it released, she checked her pad of paper. The contractions were getting closer together. A few more minutes and she was going to have to get Jack up.

She relaxed against the pillows once more. This was the last time she was going to be so alone with her baby. In a few hours, the whole world would have him. And most especially Jack's family. They were going to be thrilled to have a newborn baby in the house.

Interestingly enough, Anthony had become her

buddy of sorts. She had quickly become rather close to him. From the first day she'd come to live here at the ranch he'd taken an interest in teaching her all about the workings of the place, all about how to treat horses and cattle, how to watch for problems in the fencing, the feed, the service buildings. And at the same time, he loved talking to her about the ranch itself and what made it so special. He would come through the kitchen and give her a nod.

"Like to see a newborn calf?" he'd ask gruffly. Or perhaps it would be the new buds on the plum trees, or a basket of kittens in the barn.

"I'd love to," she'd say, and then she'd be following him across the field while he started off on a new lesson, weaving it into a history about the "Old Men" and what it had been like when they had roamed these green hills and fields.

She loved hearing the old stories and thinking that her son was going to be a part of all this. And through listening, she'd come to understand something of the depth of the man's sadness in losing his oldest son. She'd also come to realize how much he regretted his daughter moving too far away to comfortably visit, and his only remaining son turning his back on the ranch to carve out a career doing something different.

"Jack loves this ranch," she told him when he expressed his regrets to her. "I'm sure you could work something out with him. Why don't you talk to him about it?"

"Oh no." Anthony dismissed the thought with a wave of his hand. "He has his life, his business in Rio de Oro. He's worked very hard to build up that business. I couldn't ask him to leave it now. It's too late. I'm going to have to think about selling."

"Selling?" The very idea filled her with horror.

"Unless…" He gave her a significant look. "Unless your baby wants to take over when he grows up."

"Oh." There it was again, the question of succession. "I don't know.…"

But he wouldn't discuss it any further. It was obvious he thought that, barring her son's chances, the Marins were finished as a dynasty. That, she decided, was part of what caused the sadness in his dark eyes.

Jack didn't want to talk about it any more than Anthony did.

"It's up to him," he told her shortly when she tried to broach the subject. "It's his ranch. I can't interfere with his plans."

She was beginning to understand that both men were hurt, and she had no idea how to heal the wound in their relationship. But she had a feeling—irrational though it might be—that when Mikey was born, things would change. Having a baby boy in the family would make a difference. It had to.

And that brought up the issue of the name. Jack hadn't said anything about it, and yet she was as certain as she could be that he was going to ask her to name the baby Anthony when he was finally born. The only thing she wasn't certain of was what her answer was going to be. A part of her rebelled. She'd already named him Michael, darn it all. But another part wanted to do anything she could to help heal the rift and bring happiness to this family. It seemed the least she could do. Still, when he did ask, was her first reaction going to be resentment? It was possible. Because his doing that would prove he'd only married her in order to have another "Anthony." Wouldn't it?

And now here was Mikey complicating things, coming in a few days ahead of schedule, and before Jack had taken the time to ask her about the name or to tell his family the truth about the baby's conception. She didn't know any better than Jack seemed to how that should be done. It was going to be a shock. Whatever his plans were along those lines, they were going to have to wait. This baby was knocking on the door. They were going to have to let him in, no matter what his name was.

She blew air out in little puffs during another contraction, and when it was over, she pulled herself up out of bed and started for Jack's room. It was time he joined this little waiting party. He'd had a little bag packed for days, prepared with a bottle of water and snacks to keep his strength up while he kept her company during the labor period. Oh, and a book of elephant jokes. He planned to read them all to her.

"Why did the baby elephants get kicked out of the swimming pool...? Because they couldn't hold their trunks up!"

She planned to ignore them utterly.

"Don't push! Don't push!"

The nurses were rushing her toward the delivery room on a gurney.

"I'm not going to be able to hold it back much longer," Gayle cried out, then went back to intensive panting, trying to hold back the urge that filled her entire body, the urge to expel this baby as quickly as possible.

"Stay strong," Jack said encouragingly, striding alongside the gurney. "It will all be over soon."

Then she was in the delivery room, with bright lights and people in white masks, the doctor saying, "Hold on, give me a minute here," and Jack—wonderful, adorable, indispensable Jack. She held his hand so tightly it was a wonder she didn't break any bones in it, and when she finally got permission from the doctor, she pushed with all her might.

"Okay, relax, and get ready to do it again."

"I can't," she cried, exhausted, lying back and gasping for breath. The only reality in this glaring world was Jack and his hand in hers.

"Sure you can," the doctor said calmly. "Okay, here we go. Get ready to take care of business."

The urge came again, a compulsion, an overwhelming need, and she gathered every bit of strength she could find and pushed.

"Here we go!" the doctor cried. "I see a head. The baby's here."

Gayle cried out from the effort, and from the joy of knowing her baby was being born. She glanced at Jack, who was gazing downward with a look of wonder on his face. She laughed softly, too tired to pull herself up to see for herself.

"He's here," she gasped, looking into Jack's face. "Oh, thank God."

"One more push and we'll have the rest of him," the doctor said encouragingly. "Here we go."

And there was her baby. She felt him arrive, saw the commotion as the doctor held him up and handed him to the nurses, then came back to finish up with her.

"Oh, Mikey," she murmured, closing her eyes with exhaustion. "You're finally here."

"Uh, Gayle…" Jack's voice trailed off and he frowned down at her.

"What?" There was something in his tone. Fear gripped her and she found the strength to pull herself up. "What? Is something wrong with him? What?"

"No, Gayle. Calm down." The doctor was looking chagrinned. "The records you brought with you when you transferred to my care said you were having a boy. Remember?"

"Yes, of course. What is it? What's wrong?"

Jack put an arm around her shoulders and laughed softly into her neck. "Gayle, darling. We're going to have to go for a different name, I'm afraid. Michael is not going to work."

Gayle shook her head, confused. He wasn't going to bring up the "Anthony" thing now, was he? She didn't have time for that. She wanted to know what was wrong with her baby.

She was up on her elbows, still staring at her child, trying to see whatever it was everyone was so surprised about. But the baby was wrapped in a cloth by now and they were poking and prodding him and testing him for all kinds of things, just as she'd been warned they would do.

"Why can't we name him Michael?" she said, still baffled.

"Because our baby is a girl," Jack replied. "How do you like the name Michelle?"

"What? A girl?" She was still confused. Why

were they confusing her this way? She was so tired. "No, I had a boy."

"Sorry, Gayle," the doctor said again, looking up from the stitches he was setting. "I'm afraid a mistake was made. You've had a bouncing baby girl. Big and beautiful. Just the way we like them."

A nurse brought the baby over and placed her on Gayle's chest. Gayle looked at her baby and tears began rolling down her cheeks.

"Gayle," Jack said, leaning close. "Are you really upset about this?"

She shook her head. "Jack, I'm so happy...."

She couldn't talk because sobs were racking her body. She wanted to laugh because they'd been fooled about the gender of the baby. She wanted to cry because Jack wasn't getting the son he'd always wanted. She wanted to sleep for three days. And she wanted to hold her baby forever and never let her go. And not in that order.

The nurse took the baby for more testing and Gayle looked at Jack. He looked tired, too.

"Jack, I'm sorry," she said simply. "I know you wanted a boy."

"Hey, girls are nice, too," he told her, smiling. "I'm perfectly happy."

But she could see by the shadows in his eyes that he was just trying to make her feel better about it all. She bit her lip and said a little prayer. *Please, please, don't let this ruin everything.*

Little girls needed daddies just as much as little boys did.

"This is the most beautiful baby there ever was." Gayle said those words with a tone of finality that brooked no disagreement. She looked down at the perfect tiny baby fingers with their little fingernails, the downy hair on the little head, the tiny feet. Michelle was only three days old, but Gayle already wondered how she had ever existed without her.

"Oh, look," she said, enchanted by the tiny bubbles the baby was blowing out of one corner of her mouth. Laughing softly, Gayle glanced up to catch Jack's eye and share this with him, but he was staring out the kitchen window, his mind a million miles away.

Her own laughter died in her throat. His face didn't have his usual happy look. She remembered, suddenly, that from his point of view, he'd lost the son he'd expected—again. She supposed it might take some time for him to reconcile himself to having a daughter instead. Not that it was purely a gender thing, she reassured herself. It was just all this nonsense about the Anthonys. Did he hold it against her? A knife stabbed through her heart and she looked away, fighting back the despair. She couldn't worry about that now. She had a baby to think of. Jack would have to work through his problem with this on his own for now.

For the next few weeks, she was so engrossed in her new baby, she hardly had time or energy to look up and notice anyone else. Everything was new, everything had to be learned, and done right. Every move was crucial. Her baby was the focus of all her mental energy for days on end.

It was only in the third week that she began to

take in the world around her again. Trudy was a big
help. She was always ready to take over and let
Gayle get some sleep, and she was just as enchanted
by the tiny infant as Gayle was herself. Anthony was
smitten, too. He made excuses to come in from working just to see how the baby was doing, to catch her
little hand with his finger, to coo over her. Most of
the time, Gayle and her child were wrapped in a co-
coon of love such as she had never imagined.

But sometime in that third week, Gayle came to
the realization that Jack still wasn't as enthralled with
this baby as she was. In fact, he'd grown more aloof
than ever. He was always gone. There seemed to be
a lot of things he had to take care of in Rio de Oro
all of a sudden, and just about as often, he had to go
all the way down to Los Angeles for some mysteri-
ous business meetings.

His inattention worried her, and she tried to en-
gage his interest, to get him to join in the fun.

"Here. Do you want to hold her?" she said at least
once a day, smiling brightly.

Sometimes he would take Michelle, looking a little
awkward, but definitely loving, and Gayle would
melt with love for him, sure that now, at last, he was
a part of their family unit.

But more often than not, he would answer, "Uh,
no thanks. I just put on this white shirt, and anyway,
I'm late for an appointment in Santa Barbara."

It was disheartening, but she didn't know what to
do about it. In the meantime, he was having quite a
few squabbles with his father. Every few days he
would come stomping into their suite of rooms with

a frown on his face, saying, "I cannot stay here while he's here."

"You had another fight with your father?" she would ask.

"Yes," he'd answer. "He's so damn bullheaded. He won't ever listen."

She would soothe his feelings and try to get him into a better mood. But she wished there was something she could do to get the two men on better terms with each other. She knew that a lot of Jack's periodic melancholy came from his family background, the emphasis on traditions, the tragedies their family had endured. If he and his father could reconcile their differences, she was sure a lot of that would evaporate.

"What is it that constantly comes between you two?" she asked him once. "Is it because you didn't stay to take over the ranch?"

He hesitated. "That's a big part of it. When I went into geology and stayed in Rio de Oro to open my own firm, he was very upset." Frowning, he tried to analyze it in a little more depth. "All the while I was growing up, Tony was the heir to the ranch. That was a given. So I knew I would have to do something else, and I developed my love for geology. Then, after Tony died, Dad just assumed I would change my goals and take over the ranch instead. And much as I love this place, I wasn't ready to commit to that at the time." He shrugged. "It was partly a rebellion, I suppose. I knew it broke his heart, but I did it anyway."

"Still, you've kept your ties to this place strong."

He nodded. "Yes. I don't regret going into business. I needed to establish an identity away from here.'' He gave her a crooked grin. ''After all, I'm not an Anthony, am I?''

What could she say to that?

Then, one day, Jack's father came to her and told her something that made her very happy.

''I'm commissioning an artist to do a painting of Jack,'' he said. ''I want to put it up with the 'Old Men'.''

''Anthony! Do you mean it?'' Gayle was sure this would go a long way toward making Jack feel better about things.

Anthony nodded, looking smug. ''You opened my eyes to a few things, Gayle. You made me see that I was being inflexible. A fool.''

''Oh, never that!''

He leaned over the bassinet and touched Michelle's cheek with his forefinger. ''And this little dickens has helped me see how much love you can have for someone who isn't even a blood relative. I couldn't adore her more if she was my real grandchild.''

Gayle's smile felt a little stiff at that point. She was glad he'd learned that lesson, but she knew at some stage he was going to have to learn the truth.

''Traditions are very important,'' he continued. ''But there are times when you have to bend like a willow or get cut down like a pole.''

Gayle reached out and gave him a big kiss on his cheek. ''This is wonderful. Jack will be so thrilled.''

Jack wasn't thrilled at all.

''What the hell is he doing that for?'' he demanded darkly. ''It's a waste of money.''

"He's doing it for you, of course."

"Well, he shouldn't." Jack scowled. "I'm not an Anthony and I'll never be one. Let him keep things the way they have always been."

She gazed at him, at a loss. "He wants to honor you."

Jack's dark gaze raked over her scathingly. "I never cared about that."

Her jaw dropped. "Oh yes you did."

He had the grace to look just a little chagrinned. "Well, maybe I did at one time. A little. But I've learned a lot in the last few months. And you know what? I just don't give a damn."

She was glad he felt he'd learned a lot. She only wished she knew what he thought the lessons had been.

"Well, don't tell him that," she said, closing her eyes to rest them before Michelle woke for her evening feeding.

Why was it that with men, you just couldn't win? Maybe Jack didn't want things to get better. Maybe he was so used to his resentments that he couldn't let them go. She didn't know the answer, but she did know that when he kissed her good-night, there was no longer a sense of anticipation, of aroused attraction. He kissed her the way he might kiss his sister. What had happened to the man who couldn't seem to keep his hands off her?

She was too tired to think it through now, though. She would try to do that later. Maybe she would be able to think of some way out of this dead end they seemed to have wandered into.

* * *

Sometime in the fourth week, Vicky stopped by to ooh and aah over Michelle, and Gayle welcomed the company. They played with the baby in her bassinet, then as she grew drowsy, they left her to doze while they had tea on the balcony.

Gayle babbled on and on about the many wonders of her three-week-old baby, and finally Vicky asked, "So, how's Jack taking to fatherhood?"

Gayle hesitated. "Well, actually…I'm not sure." She looked at Vicky in alarm, amazed she'd said it out loud. She'd been trying to hide it, even from herself. "I mean, he loves Michelle, of course," she added quickly. "It's just that he doesn't…" She shrugged, not sure how to put it.

Vicky waved away her worries. "Gayle, my dear, you are still in your postpartum period. You are liable to have wild thoughts and fears. You'll be a little emotional. I think you should just let things go for the first few months. Go with the flow, as they say. Don't make any judgments until you are thinking a little more clearly."

Gayle stifled her first reaction. She didn't appreciate being called emotional. "You haven't seen him," she said defensively. "He doesn't even want to hold her." *Or me,* she could have added. But if she said that, she might not be able to blink back the tears quickly enough.

"Gayle, you stop worrying about that right now," Vicky scolded. "I've done this OB stuff for quite a few years now, and I can tell you this. There are lots of men who don't relate to tiny babies. After all, they don't have the equipment to feed them, and watching a baby sleep is boring as heck to them. By the time she's six months or so, when she's old enough to do a little more interacting, you'll see a real change. I guarantee it. Once he can get a real response from her, he won't be able to get enough of playing with her."

Gayle wasn't so sure Vicky knew Jack as well as she thought she did. The days were packed with things to do with her baby, as far as she was concerned. She could fill hours just watching her breathe. But she supposed men weren't wired quite the same way women were. Maybe Vicky was right. Maybe.

"Give it some time. In a few months, you'll be a little more steady and ready to evaluate things a little more objectively."

Gayle had to swallow her resentment and force a smile. She knew Vicky was just trying to help. But she was beginning to feel as though no one understood what she was going through.

"You think so?" she said stiffly.

"I know so." Vicky grabbed her hand and squeezed it. "Just don't get paranoid."

Paranoid. The word made her seethe. But she got some measure of satisfaction the next day when she overheard her father-in-law talking to Trudy in the kitchen while she was coming down the hall.

"I just don't know what's got into that boy," Anthony was saying fretfully. "He should be here with Gayle, helping her take care of this baby. What's he doing, running off to town all the time? It doesn't look good. Why, you'd almost think he resented the baby, the way he acts.''

Gayle retreated silently so that they wouldn't know they had been overheard, but it did give her a small glow of comfort to know she wasn't the only one who had noticed his behavior—and thought it stunk.

A few days later, Vicky called to see how she was doing. Just before hanging up, she thought of something else.

"You know, I was thinking of calling you the other day to find out what was going on. I saw a moving van at Jack's condo, taking things from his place. Are you selling it? Because if you are, I know some people who would love to buy it.''

Gayle blinked in surprise. "How did you know they were at Jack's condo?"

"I could see them coming out the door.'' Vicky paused. "You didn't know?"

"No.'' Gayle's fingers tightened on the receiver. "Jack hasn't said anything.''

"Oh. I thought maybe you were giving up the condo and getting a house.''

"Not that I know of.''

"Oh.'' Vicky sounded a little strained. "Maybe I shouldn't have said anything.''

Or maybe it really didn't mean anything. That was what Gayle tried to tell herself all that afternoon. And then she got another strange telephone call. The phone rang and she answered it.

"Jack Marin, please.''

"He's not here right now. This is his wife. May I take a message?"

"Hi. This is Grant Garber at Rio Escrow. This is about that house he's buying in Santa Barbara. I just need him to come in and give me a few signatures."

Gayle was speechless, but that was all right, because the man seemed to have found Jack's number.

"Oh, hey, here's his work number, the one I was supposed to call. I'll give him a buzz at this one. Sorry to have bothered you, Mrs. Marin."

"No problem," she said faintly as she hung up the receiver. Her fingers were shaking. Jack was buying a house in Santa Barbara? He hadn't said a thing to her about buying a house. And why in Santa Barbara?

Maybe, a little devilish voice said deep inside her, *Maybe he wants to put you there. Near enough to take care of, but far enough away so as not to be a bother. Why not? After all, you didn't come through with the son he wanted.*

"That's just crazy," she said aloud. And it was. But she couldn't get it out of her head.

She waited that evening for Jack to say something and clear it all up. But he didn't say a word. And every hour that passed without his explanation grew darker and darker.

He seemed distracted during dinner. He barely looked at Michelle and barely spoke to anyone else. After eating, he sat in front of the television, staring at it, though the program was idiotic.

"Come here and say good-night to your daughter," Gayle told him as she was getting the sweet little thing ready for bed. She had her decked out in a pink sleeper with a little red bow, and the baby looked adorable. She had a new trick of pursing her lips and giving what looked like little fish kisses to the air. Michelle was a baby any daddy would love. Gayle looked up expectantly as Jack neared them. How could he resist this little bundle of joy?

"Night, sweetheart," he said, giving the baby a half smile and chucking her under the chin. And then his attention was back on the television screen.

Gayle stood staring at him, her heart heavy. Michelle began to squirm, and she held her closely as she carried her into the bedroom. Gayle knew now that she wasn't being paranoid. Jack was definitely losing interest in them. There was no doubt about it.

"I don't know what's wrong with your daddy, baby mine," she murmured as she rocked Michelle in her arms.

You fool, the little voice said. *He never wanted a daughter. He wanted a son. That was the whole point and purpose of everything he's done.*

A dreadful sorrow was welling up in her. She was beginning to be afraid that the annoying little voice was right. Maybe she wasn't going to be able to stay.

Chapter Eleven

Gayle's dark skies suddenly showed a silver lining. Anthony and Trudy were going up to Paso Robles for the weekend, visiting Jana and her family. Two long days and two long nights alone with Jack... Her heart beat faster just thinking about it. This was it. Jack had called to say he was coming home early this afternoon. She was going to have a chance to make a final stand at drawing him closer. She was going to seduce him back into this relationship. Her mind raced with plans, and she was filled with optimism. He'd wooed her into this marriage, now she was going to woo him to renew that commitment.

Every time she felt hopeless about their situation, all she had to do was see his handsome face and she was reminded of the night they had slept together in his bed. She'd never felt closer to any other man. She yearned to have the closeness again. But it looked as if her only chance of getting it would come from being proactive. Just waiting around for things to change wasn't working.

She fed Michelle and put her down, only to have her wake up again, fussing. Gayle picked her up to rock her, and thought she felt a little warm, but decided that was just because she'd been crying for a few moments before she'd gotten to her. A few minutes of pacing the floor with her baby on her shoulder were all that was needed. Michelle was fast asleep, and Gayle laid her down and turned away, ready to prepare for an afternoon rendezvous with her husband.

"Tonight," she whispered to herself as she headed for the shower. "Tonight is the night."

Jack walked into the house and knew something was different right away. It just didn't seem the same. Where pungent cooking smells usually met him there was instead the scent of spring flowers. And instead of Trudy's usual Frank Sinatra tunes, he thought he heard Andrea Bocelli playing in the background. He was turning slowly, surveying with a frown the house he'd grown up in and thought he knew, when a voice came from behind him.

"Hi."

He turned and, for a split second, wasn't sure who was coming toward him.

So far he'd known two Gayles. There was the very pregnant Gayle, a woman who was a wary friend, and then a close companion, a woman who aroused him even though that wouldn't have seemed possible. He'd liked that Gayle a lot—in fact, he'd married her—but she'd pretty much disappeared when the baby was born.

Suddenly he'd been confronted with a thinner, but less attentive woman, someone who wore baggy clothes and forgot to comb her hair, who always appeared with a baby on her shoulder or at least milk stains on her blouse. For the first couple of weeks he'd had the impression this Gayle didn't really remember who he was or why he might be showing up in her suite of rooms at night. Luckily, his work load had increased at about the same time the transformation had occurred, so he hadn't been around much.

Now there was a completely new Gayle in his house. He gaped at her, liking what he saw. This Gayle had combed her hair into soft waves around her shoulders, and she was wearing a little black dress that seemed to show off curves he hadn't even known she had. Her smile was different, too. She seemed to be seeing him, taking him in body and soul, evaluating him as a man in a way that sent his pulse rate soaring.

"Wow," he said, noting the swell of her breasts just where the fabric turned lacy; the curve of her hips, looking like an excellent place for him to put his hands; the length of her very shapely legs. "You look…"

"Sexy?" she suggested when he hesitated. She stopped in front of him and smiled up into his eyes. "That was the look I was going for."

He nodded, then groaned. "Gayle, this isn't fair," he said huskily. "We're in this damn marriage of convenience, remember?"

"Uh-uh." She shook her head. "I don't remember that at all." Reaching up, she hooked her arms around his neck. "I do remember someone promising to take me as his loving wife." She arched her body against his.

His breathing was coming very fast now, and his slacks were getting ridiculously uncomfortable. "Gayle, you know we can't do anything until after your six-week checkup."

She smiled. "I had my checkup yesterday. What's your next excuse?"

His eyes darkened. "Where are Trudy and my dad?" he asked, then realized he was following the very pattern she was teasing him about.

"Gone to Jana's. You knew they were going."

"Did I?" If he'd had any idea he was going to be coming home to this, he would have come home hours ago. He was beginning to feel light-headed. "The baby?" he asked breathlessly, his gaze focusing on her lush, beautiful mouth.

"Asleep. She should be good for at least an hour."

"Then you and I...?"

"Have time to ourselves." Her smile was a silky invitation to sensual delight. "What do you think we should do with it?"

There was no point in talking. They both knew the answer, and as his mouth began to devour hers, his hands slid down her sides and found her hips, pulling her firmly into the hard, solid heat of his. He'd been dreaming about making love to her since the day they'd met. He'd been holding back, agonizing over the frustration, but doing his duty. And now he was free to let her know, with the hunger of his body, just how he felt about her. He lifted her again, as he had done so often when she was pregnant, and this time she was lighter than air. He carried her to the bed, his breath ragged in his throat. Her clothes seemed to dissolve away, and he ripped his own aside. She seemed to melt under his hands and he whispered words into her hair as they came together, loving words that came out sounding harsh when he meant to express his tenderness. But the wait had been too long, and his urgency was as fierce as the surge of the ocean. And afterward, as they lay tangled together on the rumpled sheets, he wondered if she'd understood what he was trying to say with his lovemaking.

She touched his face and talked softly. He took in her golden body and felt as though he had everything he'd ever wanted. They kissed, made love again and laughed at each other. For almost an hour, everything was perfect.

And then he remembered that he had to go. He'd only come home to pack a suitcase. He'd forgotten to tell her that.

Gayle sat on the bed and watched him dress. She'd just gone from the ecstasy of making love in a way she'd never known before, to the depths of despair once again. Jack was leaving. He'd made love to her, made her feel as though she were flying, and now he was going away. He was saying over and over how sorry he was, and how much this had meant to him, but she didn't believe it any longer. She'd put herself on the line tonight. She'd opened her heart and her longing, and showed him all her cards.

"I forgot to tell you," he'd told her just moments before. "I'm going to have to go to Los Angeles for a couple of days."

For a couple of days. For the couple of days she'd thought they would have together.

"What for?" she asked, her voice strained.

"I've got to finalize some business deals I've been working on. Tie up some loose ends."

His tone was evasive, and that really twisted the knife. Why was he acting like this? "What kind of business deals?"

He actually had the nerve to smile at her. "Never mind. All in good time."

She clenched her jaw, then tried to remain calm as she added, "You never tell me what anything is about anymore. I feel like you are more and more remote from me. Like you're living some kind of other life out there."

He laughed, looking in the mirror as he tied his tie. "They say new mothers are paranoid. I guess they're right." He gave the tie a jerk and centered it. "Just stay calm. You'll find out what this is all about soon enough."

Paranoid. How she hated that word! It was unfair, just a red herring to keep her from seeming to have legitimate complaints. "Oh, don't listen to Gayle, she's just being paranoid."

The word made her furious. He kissed her again before going out the door, but she didn't kiss him back. She was so angry, she didn't know where to turn. She had laid herself open to him, handed him her heart, and he didn't have time to accept it, because he had a business meeting.

She wanted to throw something. Smash some furniture. Scream. But those things weren't really her style. Still, she had to do something. One thing she knew was that she wasn't going to do was stay here in his house anymore. She wasn't going to hang around, begging for scraps from the man she loved. She was out of here.

Rushing into Michelle's bedroom, she began to pack her things. She and her baby were hitting the road.

"Better to leave when your welcome has just expired," she told herself, "than to wait around to get your walking papers."

So he thought he was going to set her up in a house in Santa Barbara, did he? Well, she would just see about that. She still had her old place in Rio de Oro. The baby room was still set up. If she went back, it would be just as though she'd never found Jack, as though things were back on the trajectory they'd been on before he'd come into her life. So what would she have lost?

Nothing but your heart, that annoying voice inside told her. But she shook it off. Letting her heart become involved had been her first mistake. She wouldn't do that again.

She lifted Michelle from her bassinet and frowned. The baby definitely felt warm, and that worried her. But Vicky was in town today. Gayle would swing by Vicky's office and ask her opinion before calling the pediatrician. Feeling better about the situation, she dressed her little girl for travel and put her in the car seat. They were going to have to drive in her old blue compact, the car Jack had ordered her never to put Michelle in. Gayle had a qualm about that, but what the heck. The car had never let her down in all these years. One more trip wouldn't hurt. In a few minutes, they were on the road, headed for Rio de Oro. In less than an hour, she would be back in her own apartment. What a relief.

Traffic was bad and it actually took over an hour to make it back. She dropped by Vicky's office, but no one was there, so Gayle went on to her own place, planning to try calling her pediatrician from there. By the time she'd unpacked Michelle from the car, she was genuinely worried. Her daughter's face was brightly flushed and her skin was hot to the touch. Suddenly, there was no choice at all. She knew what she had to do. Packing her right back into the car seat, she set off for the hospital. Michelle was definitely sick. Gayle only hoped she hadn't waited too long to do something about it.

"Hang in there, baby girl," she murmured as Michelle began to fuss. "Everything's going to be okay."

Glancing back at her child, she felt dread building in her heart. Everything else seemed to want to go wrong in her life. What if...?

"Please, please," she prayed softly. "Please let Michelle be okay."

Jack's L.A. meeting was just breaking up when he got the phone call. He was in the law offices of Sherwin and Gomberg, shaking hands with the attorneys and the representatives from TriTerraCorp, and there were smiles all around. Negotiations were finally concluded. He'd sold his environmental study firm,

Earth Matters, Incorporated, to TriTerraCorp, and managed to get a great deal for his employees in the bargain. That had been the main sticking point. There was no way he would have gone through with the deal if it was going to leave his long-time employees, the people who had been loyal to him from the beginning, in the lurch. But now they were guaranteed their jobs, plus good option plans for TriTerraCorp stock and better retirement benefits than he had been able to provide. A huge weight was off his shoulders.

And then the call came through.

"Message for you. It's your secretary."

"At this time of night?" He took the receiver from the lawyer who held it. "Hello?" he said.

"Mr. Marin? It's Betty." Her voice sounded anxious. "Did Vicky get in touch with you?"

His danger-response adrenaline began to rush. "No. Why?" he snapped.

"Well, I'm not sure. I came by the office to pick up some papers and there was a message on my machine. Vicky said she was looking for you. Something about Gayle and Michelle being at the hospital...."

The lights seemed to dim. "What happened?" he demanded hoarsely.

"I don't know. I've tried to call her back, but she's not answering."

"Santa Ynez Hospital?"

"No! The hospital here in Rio de Oro. At least, that was what she said...."

"I'll be there as fast as I can."

"I'll go over and—"

Betty's words were cut off as he slammed down

the phone and turned to run for the door. In another three minutes, he was on the freeway, heading north. It would take him a little over an hour if he kept to the speed limit. He figured he would make it in about forty minutes.

Making that kind of time, he was going to need all his concentration on his driving. The picture in his mind was of Gayle's old blue car. His hands gripped the wheel and he stared straight ahead, but he allowed one part of his attention to divert for a few moments while he whispered a desperate prayer.

Gayle was using the telephone at the back of the lobby of the small-town hospital when Jack came rushing in, and he didn't see her. He went to the desk, barking out, "Gayle Marin and baby Michelle? Where are they?"

The receptionist smiled and barely had time to say, "Room 213—" before he was sprinting off down the hall. Gayle jumped up and had to hurry to keep him in sight. By the time she got to the room, he was inside, leaning over their baby.

"Is she okay?" he was asking the nurse, his voice higher than usual. "Why is she so red? What's happened?"

"She's sick, poor baby," the older woman told him calmly. "But it's only—"

"Sick? What do you mean, sick? She's not hurt?"

The nurse smiled indulgently. "No, Mr. Marin. She's got roseola, a very common childhood disease. Her temperature will be high for a couple of days, but she's going to be fine."

His shoulders seemed to sag. "Oh. Thank God." Then he straightened. "Where's Gayle?"

"Right here, Jack," she said from behind him, as the nurse discreetly left the room.

He whirled, and she waited, not sure what to expect from him. Recriminations? Questions? Anger? He had a right to wonder why she was so far from where he'd left her.

But she got none of that. Instead, he erased the space between them in one stride and took her in his arms, holding her close to his chest and breathing into her hair.

"Thank God you're okay," he murmured. "You don't know what nightmare scenarios I was imagining as I was driving up here. I thought you might have been in a car accident. I was so scared...." Pulling back, he took her face in his hands and rained kisses down on her cheek, her ear, her nose.

"Jack, stop," she cried, laughing. But she loved every minute of it. Had he really said what she'd thought she heard?

"You're sure Michelle is all right?" he demanded.

She nodded. "They tell me roseola is very common and not very dangerous, but her fever is high and they wanted to keep her overnight, just to be safe."

He let his breath out in a long sigh. "Thank God. Did you see Vicky?"

"She's been here. I had a heck of a time finding her. We played phone and page tag for the longest time. Oh, and Betty came by. She told me she'd been in touch with you, so I knew you were coming."

"But...why are you here?" he asked, gazing

down into her eyes. "Why aren't you at the Santa Ynez hospital?"

"Because..." She hesitated, not sure how she was going to explain this one gracefully. "I moved back to my apartment."

He stared at her blankly. "You did what?"

She lifted her chin defiantly. "I packed up my things and packed up Michelle and I moved out."

He was completely baffled, shaking his head as though she were speaking in a Tibetan dialect he couldn't understand. "Why?"

She drew herself up and met his gaze levelly. "Because I was tired of begging to get your attention."

"What are you talking about?"

"Jack, you've been gone so much—and when you're home, you're mind is usually a million miles away." She searched his eyes, wondering if he could understand. "I may be crazy, Jack, but...I love you. I love you so much...." Her voice choked and tears brimmed in her eyes. "I can't stand that you don't love me that way. I'd rather get out of your life than to—"

He grabbed her by the shoulders, looking like he was going to shake her. "What are you talking about? Gayle, I'm nuts about you. Can't you tell?"

He was a shimmering figure through her tears. "You...you are?"

"Yes, I am." He said it almost as though the fact really annoyed him. "I'm so nuts about you—and that baby—that I've spent the last few weeks negotiating the sale of my business to TriTerraCorp."

She stared him, her mouth gaping. "You sold Earth Matters?"

He nodded. "Got a great price, too. I wanted to make it possible for us to live on the ranch while we raise our kids. And I did it." He was proud of that fact, and it showed.

"You mean…"

"I'm planning to ease Anthony out and take over most of the operations myself, with the help of a foreman. I want to leave some time to do research on the environmental impact text I'm planning to write with a colleague who teaches at Stanford University. But I'll have plenty of time to devote to you and Michelle from now on. My business trips are over."

She shook her head, trying hard to come to grips with what he was saying. "But what about the house in Santa Barbara? What about the moving van clearing out your place in town?"

He cocked an eyebrow and grimaced. "So you heard about those things. I swear, you can't keep a secret in that town." He sighed. "The moving van was just to clear out all the boy things in the baby room. I thought I'd put them in storage until we need them. And the house… Don't tell Anthony. It's a surprise for him."

She shook her head, still at sea. "What is?"

"The house in Santa Barbara. I got it for him and Trudy. They've always talked about how they would like to retire there, and I made it possible for them to do it now."

She took a deep breath. "Oh Jack, you and your surprises. Why didn't you tell me all this?"

His face was innocent as a child's. "Because then it wouldn't be a surprise."

She laughed softly, snuggling against his chest. "Okay, Jack. That's the first thing that's going to change." She looked up at him. "If you had just told me you were doing these things, I could have avoided so much worry. We are a unit now, you and I. We should plan surprises together."

He looked down into her face in wonder. "You're right. And if you had only told me what you were worried about..."

She sighed. Why hadn't she thought of that? It seemed they both were going to have to work a little harder at making the adjustment from being individuals to being a team. "You're right. It works both ways." She paused. "I thought you were backing out of the marriage because we had a girl—not a boy," she confessed.

He looked at her incredulously. "Are you out of your mind? I love you and Michelle more than anything in the world."

Then he kissed her. She rose to his kiss, like a flower to the sun, and tasted his love, really recognizing it for the first time.

"We are a unit now, aren't we?" he murmured against her skin.

"Yes."

"Together." He raised their joined hands and looked at them. Their wedding rings shone in the lamplight. "That's you and me."

"And Michelle," she reminded him.

He grinned, looking over at the hospital bed. "And Michelle," he declared.

Epilogue

Six months later

Gayle came up the stairs to their suite of rooms to find Jack feeding cereal to Michelle, who was lolling in her wooden high chair.

"Jack, come on down here and see this," she said from the stairway. "Your father has your portrait and he's going to hang it in the library."

He popped another mouthful of cereal into Michelle's little mouth and looked up at Gayle. "Does he have the others, too?"

"What others?"

"When he brought it up last month I told him not to bother to hang mine unless he had one of you, and one of this little rascal." He chucked Michelle under her chin, making her giggle. "We're a family unit, remember?"

"I suppose he's got them, then, because the package looked awfully large for one painting." She came in and leaned beside him, smiling at her adorable baby girl. Gayle couldn't believe how much she'd grown in just six months. It seemed like a miracle.

True to his word, Jack had moved all his operations home with a vengeance. He and Anthony spent the mornings out working the ranch while she cared for Michelle. Some afternoons, he did his research while she read or visited with friends. Other afternoons, they packed Michelle up and went for rides into the country, or to the lake, or to the beach. All in all, it was an idyllic life. Almost—but not quite—too good to be true.

Anthony and Trudy had been shocked but quickly thrilled, to learn that Michelle was Jack's biological child. They had made plans to move to the Santa Barbara house for part of every year, but they hadn't quite made the break yet and were still at the ranch for the time being. And that was just as well, Gayle thought, because Michelle would miss them if they weren't around to be her adoring audience for every new trick.

"Okay," Jack said, giving his little girl another spoonful of cereal. "I'll come down just as soon as Michelle finishes eating. I want to fill her up so she'll go to bed early." He gave his wife a significant look. "Anthony and Trudy are taking in a movie tonight. We'll have the place to ourselves."

"Will we?" She laughed at his obvious intentions and hugged to herself the warm feeling he conjured up inside her. The best thing she'd ever done was make a mistake in the baby-making process. If she hadn't met Jack... But that didn't bear thinking about.

"Dad will need help getting the pictures hung straight," Jack continued. "And I want to make sure he leaves room for the rest of them."

"The rest of them?" Gayle looked at him, bemused. "Who is 'the rest of them'?"

He looked up at her, his eyes full of mischief. "The six or seven other children we're going to have, of course."

"Six or seven?" She pretended to blanch. "The number keeps getting higher all the time." She patted her tummy. "And this little one is only a few weeks old. Stop counting your children before they're hatched." She turned to go back down. "I'll tell him you're coming," she said, throwing back a flirtatious smile that he caught and returned.

Michelle took this opportunity to flip the cereal bowl up on her head like a silly hat. Rivulets of wet cereal poured down her face. She laughed up into her father's eyes, charmed with her own trick, and he laughed right back.

Gayle stood in the doorway, shaking her head as she watched the two of them communicate. And to think that she had once worried that he wasn't bonding with his child. The little darling already knew who to go to for any indulgence whatsoever. Michelle had her daddy wrapped around her finger.

"Talk about a daddy's girl," she muttered, watching them with love. She picked up a damp cloth and began cleaning the mess her daughter had made. Jack took off her "hat" and pulled her out of the high chair and cuddled her in his arms.

"Let's go down and see the pictures," he cooed to her. "Ready, big girl?"

She babbled nonsense at him, looking very pleased with herself. Grabbing his nose, she let out a squeal of delight, and then said, "Da Da."

Jack stopped dead, looking down at his girl, then up at his wife. "Did you hear that? Did you hear it? She said 'Da Da.'"

"Really?" Gayle teased. "And who the heck is Da Da?"

"That's me," he said emphatically, looking wounded that she would quibble about such an honor.

"Nobody around here calls you Da Da. Why would she do it?"

"Because she's the smartest baby there ever was," he said, holding her close as he started down the stairs. "And she knows her Da Da."

Gayle laughed. "This little one better be a son," she noted as she followed them. "I need somebody on my side."

Jack turned and caught her as she reached the bottom, pulling her into their little group. "I'm always on your side," he told her softly, looking into her eyes as though he could see her heart there.

She lifted her face for his kiss. "I know," she whispered to him, her eyes shining. "We're a family unit."

"Da Da!" Michelle called out a few moments later.

"You see?" Jack exclaimed. "She said it again. She knows!"

Gayle laughed and they walked toward the library arm in arm. A family unit. What could be better?

* * * * *

Don't miss the reprisal of Silhouette Romance's popular miniseries

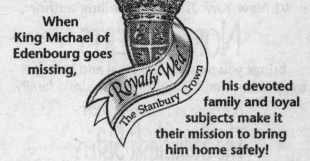

When King Michael of Edenbourg goes missing, his devoted family and loyal subjects make it their mission to bring him home safely!

Royally Wed

The Stanbury Crown

Their search begins March 2001 and continues through June 2001.

On sale March 2001: **THE EXPECTANT PRINCESS**
by bestselling author **Stella Bagwell** (SR #1504)

On sale April 2001: **THE BLACKSHEEP PRINCE'S BRIDE**
by rising star **Martha Shields** (SR #1510)

On sale May 2001: **CODE NAME: PRINCE**
by popular author **Valerie Parv** (SR #1516)

On sale June 2001: **AN OFFICER AND A PRINCESS**
by award-winning author **Carla Cassidy** (SR #1522)

Available at your favorite retail outlet.

Silhouette®

Where love comes alive™

#1 *New York Times* bestselling author

NORA ROBERTS

brings you more of the loyal and loving,
tempestuous and tantalizing Stanislaski family.

Coming in February 2001

The Stanislaski Sisters

Natasha and Rachel

Though raised in the Old World traditions of their
family, fiery Natasha Stanislaski and cool, classy
Rachel Stanislaski are ready for a *new* world of love....

*And also available in February 2001 from
Silhouette Special Edition, the newest book in the
heartwarming Stanislaski saga*

CONSIDERING KATE

Natasha and Spencer Kimball's daughter Kate turns her
back on old dreams and returns to her hometown, where
she finds the *man* of her dreams.

Available at your favorite retail outlet.

Where love comes alive™

MAITLAND MATERNITY

Where the luckiest babies are born!

In March 2001, look for

BILLION DOLLAR BRIDE
by Muriel Jensen

**Billionaire Austin Cahill doesn't believe
in love or marriage—**

he only wants to marry in order to produce an heir. Single
mom and wedding planner Anna Maitland is horrified by his
old-fashioned attitude. So when Austin proposes a marriage
of convenience, will Anna be able to refuse him...
now that she's fallen in love with him?

*Each book tells a different story about the
world-renowned Maitland Maternity Clinic—
where romances are born, secrets are revealed...
and bundles of joy are delivered.*

HARLEQUIN®
Makes any time special ™

Silhouette®
Where love comes alive™

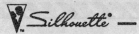

100th BOOK

Join Silhouette Books as
award-winning, bestselling author

Marie Ferrarella

celebrates her 100th Silhouette title!

Don't miss
ROUGH AROUND THE EDGES
Silhouette Romance #1505
March 2001

To remain in the United States, Shawn O'Rourke
needed a wife. Kitt Dawson needed a home
for herself and the baby daughter Shawn
had helped her deliver. A marriage of
convenience seemed the perfect solution—
until they discovered that the real thing was
much more appealing than playacting....

Available at your favorite retail outlet.

Silhouette®
Where love comes alive™

International Bestselling Author

DIANA PALMER

At eighteen, Amanda Carson left
west Texas, family scandal and a man
she was determined to forget. But the Whitehall
empire was vast, and when the powerful family wanted
something, they got it. Now they wanted Amanda—and her
advertising agency. Jace Whitehall, a man Amanda hated and
desired equally, was waiting to finish what began years ago.
Now they must confront searing truths about both their
families. And the very thing that drove Amanda from this
land might be the only thing able to keep her there.

THE Cowboy AND THE Lady

"Nobody tops Diana Palmer."
—Jayne Ann Krentz

Available February 2001 wherever paperbacks are sold!